BLOODY KNUCKLES 3

THERE WILL BE BLOOD

Copyright © 2024 Tranay Adams/ BLOODY KNUCKLES 3

Published by Dope Readz Presents

All rights reserved. No part of this book may be reproduced in any form without the written consent of the publisher, except for brief quotes used in reviews.

This is a work of fiction. Any references or similarities to actual events, real people, living or dead, or real locals are intended to give the novel a sense of reality. Any similarity in other names, characters, places, and incidents is entirely coincidental.

BLOODY KNUCKLES 3
A Novel by *Tranay Adams*

Table of Contents

PROLOGUE 5
Chapter one 12
Chapter two 18
Chapter three 23
Chapter four 29
Chapter five 34
Chapter six 39
Chapter seven 46
Chapter eight 53
Chapter nine 61
Chapter ten 70
Chapter eleven 78
Chapter twelve 85
Chapter thirteen 94
Chapter fourteen 103
Chapter fifteen 112
Chapter sixteen 120
Chapter seventeen 128
Chapter eighteen 135
Chapter nineteen 142
Chapter twenty 150
Chapter twenty-one 159
Chapter twenty-two 169

PROLOGUE

LaDecia lay on the hard cot, her body trembling as she prepared to execute their desperate plan. She could hear the distant murmur of guards and the occasional clink of metal from the lone prisoner in the cell next to hers—Luka, her man. Taking a deep breath, she began to convulse, her eyes rolling back as froth formed at her mouth. The guard stationed outside her cell glanced over, alarmed, and quickly unlocked the door, rushing in to help.

"LaDecia, can you hear me?" he shouted, panic evident in his voice. As he turned to call for backup, LaDecia's eyes snapped open. She kneed him in the stomach, and as he doubled over, she slammed his face into the wall with all her strength. He crumpled to the floor, unconscious.

Quickly, she grabbed his rifle and checked its ammunition. She also took his 8-shot revolver and tucked it into her waistband. Stepping out of her cell, she moved silently, shooting down a second guard before he could react. She swiftly unlocked Luka's cell and handed him the revolver.

"Are you okay?" she whispered, her eyes scanning the corridor.

"I am now," Luka replied, taking the revolver. He used a broken piece of mirror to watch their backs through the cell bars. Suddenly, he spotted a third guard approaching. With a calm, practiced motion, he fired two shots, each finding their mark. The guard grumbled in pain as he fell to his death.

A distant clanking sound echoed through the corridors. Luka's heart raced as he realized the source. "Hyenas," he muttered. Through the back entrance of the homemade jail, a fourth guard released two snarling beasts, their eyes wild and mouths foaming.

Luka acted quickly. He tossed two rotten steaks rubbed down with Ambien into his cell. The hyenas, driven by hunger, ran inside to devour the meat. Luka slammed the cell door shut behind them, trapping the beasts.

"Go through the front door and circle around to the back," Luka whispered to LaDecia. He kissed her quickly before she moved away. He hoisted one of the dead guards up. Using him as a human shield, he kicked open the back door.

The last guard opened fire, his bullets thudding into the lifeless body. Luka fired two shots, but they went wide. He pushed the human shield out of the door and ducked back inside.

A single gunshot rang out—Blat! The guard fell to the ground and revealed LaDecia standing behind him, her assault rifle smoking. She whistled for Luka to come outside. As soon as he joined her, they heard a vehicle approaching.

"Quickly, we need to hide the bodies," LaDecia said. They dragged the dead guards inside and stashed them in her cell. Just as they finished, Demonte, the camp leader, and another guard stepped inside the jail.

Luka moved swiftly, blowing the guard's face off and pressing his revolver against Demonte's nose. LaDecia stood beside him, her assault rifle trained on Demonte.

"Take us to your office and open the safe," Luka demanded with an icy voice.

Demonte, visibly afraid, nodded and led them to his office. With shaky hands, he opened the safe, revealing passports, identification cards, birth certificates, thirty thousand in Brazilian currency, and the bill of sale forms for all the children they had been forced to breed.

LaDecia's eyes filled with tears as she saw the documents. She covered her mouth, sobs wracking her body. "These are our children," she whispered. "They sold our children."

Luka held her tightly. "We'll find them," he vowed. "We'll find every last one of them and bring them home."

Determination burned in their eyes as they gathered the documents. They knew their fight was far from over, but together, they had the strength to take on whatever came next. As they prepared to leave, Luka turned to Demonte, his expression hardening.

"You're going to help us," he said. "Or you'll end up like your guards."

Demonte nodded vigorously, fear evident in his eyes. "I'll do whatever you want," he stammered.

LaDecia looked at the man who had caused them so much pain. "Then start talking," she said, her voice cold. "Tell us where our children are."

Luka held up the stack of Brazilian money before Demonte's eyes. "I know this is just a decoy for thieves should they stick this shithole up. I've seen you bring in reais by the boatload, so where is the rest?"

"I—" Demonte's lie died in his throat by a wicked smack to the mouth. Blood trickled down his lip as Luka smacked him repeatedly.

"Don't chu even think about lying to me, or I swear to Christ I'll beat chu to death with my bare hands!" Luka snarled, smacking him in the mouth with the money, causing bills to fly everywhere.

Demonte, mad dogging him, licked the blood off his lips and muttered, "The money is all around you."

Luka and LaDecia's eyes darted to the ceiling, the walls, and then the floor. Luka stomped the floorboards and dust rose. He motioned for LaDecia to step back, then busted up the boards with the butt of his pistol. As he began pulling up the broken floorboards, he found money wrapped in clear plastic. Smiling, he tore open the plastic and grabbed some of the money out, checking its authenticity. He handed the money to LaDecia, who confirmed it was real.

He took her assault rifle and began busting out the walls, revealing more hidden cash. Knocking everything off Demonte's desk, he climbed up on it and started making holes in the ceiling with the butt of the rifle. Switching hands with the weapon, he used the other to pull the hole open further. He narrowed his eyes as debris trickled down. "Jackpot," Luka grinned at LaDecia, holding up the money he'd taken from the ceiling.

Luka jumped down to the floor, punching Demonte in the chin, and knocking him out cold. He gave LaDecia back her weapon, yanked the telephone cord out of the wall, and tied Demonte up with it.

LaDecia stripped down to her bra and Luka stripped down to his bare chest. Together, they loaded all of Demonte's money into the cargo van he had driven back to the camp.

***

Demonte awoke groaning and blinking his eyes. His soul nearly leaped from his body when he realized he was locked up with the hyenas. The beasts approached him as they licked their razor-sharp teeth.

"Aaaaaaaaah!"

***

LaDecia and Luka heard Demonte's screams as they drove off the grounds of the incarceration camp he'd built. Luka, behind the wheel, looked over at LaDecia, who was poring over the bill of sales for their children. She couldn't remember what they all looked like when they were born, but she was thankful Luka had come up with the idea of marking them at birth in hopes of locating them in the future. The upright L and the upside-down L, which were her and Luka's initials, came to her mind vividly.

"We'll find them," Luka assured her, gripping the steering wheel tightly. "We'll find them and we'll bring them all home."

Tears streamed down LaDecia's face as she looked over the bill of sale documents, each one was a lifeline to their lost children. Demonte had listed the children as pups on the forms, but LaDecia and Luka named them at birth.

Luka and LaDecia had taken the first step toward reuniting their family. The fight was far from over, but together, they would face whatever challenges lay ahead.

CHAPTER ONE

Wild Child, his cornrows frizzy and his hands encased in fingerless black gloves, stood before one of the wall-to-wall mirrors inside the dojo. He examined the scars on his shoulder, the unique marks his father, Luka, had given him at birth. They always drew curiosity from others, but he simply referred to them as his "birthmarks." The truth, unbeknownst to him, was far more complicated and painful.

"Yoooooo," a voice rang out from across the dojo, snapping Wild Child out of his thoughts. He turned to see his trainer McGuiness, a slender white man wearing a red headband and a dingy black gi, standing with a commanding presence.

"Time to get back to work, pretty boy. Let's go," McGuiness called, motioning him over.

Wild Child nodded, the intensity returning to his eyes. He dashed across the dojo's mat, his bare feet slapping softly against the smooth surface. Purp and Stutter-Box stood watching in the background.

McGuiness didn't waste any time. "Alright, Wild Child, let's see what you've got," he said, stepping into a fighting stance.

Wild Child mirrored his trainer, his muscles tensing in anticipation. The dojo fell silent except for the faint rustle of their movements. They circled each other, eyes locked, searching for an opening.

McGuiness struck first, a swift jab aimed at Wild Child's face. Wild Child dodged effortlessly, countering with a quick strike to McGuiness's ribs. The trainer grunted, stepping back and nodding in approval.

"Good, keep that speed up," McGuiness instructed, adjusting his stance.

Wild Child, movements fluid and precise, pressed the attack, landing a series of blows, each one met with a block or dodge from McGuiness. The trainer's experience showed, but Wild Child's raw talent and determination were undeniable.

As the training session continued, McGuiness pushed Wild Child harder. "Faster! Stronger! Don't hold back!" he shouted, echoing through the dojo.

Wild Child responded with a fierce combination of kicks and punches, driving McGuiness back. Sweat dripped from their faces, their breathing heavy, but neither showed any sign of slowing down.

Purp and Stutter-Box watched intently, their expressions finally breaking into faint smiles of approval. They had seen Wild Child grow from a raw, untamed fighter into a disciplined warrior, and today was another step in his evolution.

After a grueling hour, McGuiness called for a break. "Alright, that's enough for now," he said, stepping back and wiping his forehead with a towel. "You're getting better, Wild Child. Keep this up, and you'll be unstoppable."

Wild Child nodded, panting but smiling. He glanced back at the mirror, the scars on his shoulders catching the light. They were a reminder of his past, of the pain and struggles he had endured. But they were also a symbol of his strength, of the resilience that had brought him this far.

He walked up to Purp and Stutter-Box, who clapped him on the back.

"Them hands gettin' nicer, my G," Purp complimented, his deep voice filled with pride.

"Y—yeah, you—you gon' def—definitely win that tour—tournament," Stutter-Box added, grinning. "Just—just keep pushing."

Wild Child walked away snickering and shaking his head.

***

Dark figures toting AR-15s equipped with infrared lasers hopped the gates of Liebowitz's mansion and stormed across the front lawn. The piercing ring of the security alarm echoed through the night, heightening the tension.

***

A stampede of men raced through the mansion's hallways, pistols at the ready. One of them unlocked the steel doors of the armory and opened them like refrigerator doors. He started grabbing AK-47s and round drums of ammunition, passing them out like they were sack lunches on a school field trip. When the men received their weapons, they sprinted out to defend the perimeter, loading their assault rifles.

***

Delroy raced past the influx of men in the opposite direction, pushing Liebowitz's wheelchair. The entire mansion shook under the force of explosions and rapid gunfire. The sound of glass shattering, chandeliers crashing, and furniture toppling echoed through the hallways.

Delroy rolled Liebowitz into a secret elevator hidden behind the bookshelf in his study. As soon as the doors closed, Liebowitz removed the necklace containing a red key from around his neck, slid it into a slot, and turned it. He smacked a glowing button labeled "E.S.," which stood for Escape Route. The elevator rumbled and began to descend. Delroy and Liebowitz listened to the chaos above. Liebowitz kept his Draco pointed at the doors while Delroy stood behind him, FN pinned on the entrance. They were ready to neutralize any threat that awaited them.

When the elevator doors opened, no threat was in sight. Delroy tucked his gun into his waistband and loaded Liebowitz into the dusty pearl white Cadillac Escalade parked before them. He started the SUV and activated the windshield fluid, and wipers to clean the glass. He then sped down a lit tunnel, debris falling from the ceiling due to the explosions in the mansion. Bats flew past the Escalade and tarantulas fell onto it, but Delroy paid them no mind. His main concern was getting out of there safely.

The faster Delroy drove, the larger the twin metal doors ahead appeared. He pressed a button on a device clipped to the sun visor and the doors slid apart. The Escalade emerged from the ground and landed in a wooded area. Delroy sped down a well-paved road and shortly merged into city traffic. He pulled up to a red stoplight and sighed with relief. Glancing at Liebowitz through the rearview mirror, he saw that the older man was also relieved. The traffic light turned green. Delroy went to press the gas pedal when four black-on-black H2 Hummers appeared from all directions, boxing them in.

Delroy drew his gun for another firefight but Liebowitz grabbed his shoulder. He shook his head, letting Delroy know this was a fight they couldn't win. With that, Delroy threw out his gun and exited the truck with his hands up, surrendering. He got down on his knees in the middle of the street, as several men with AR-15s approached.

CHAPTER TWO

Chyna, Bag Man, and Augustus pulled ski masks over their faces, adjusting them until they could see out of the eye holes properly. They slid on black sunglasses, the dark lenses reflecting their steely determination. Picking up their M-16 assault rifles, they stood silently, watching the numbers above the elevator doors light up one by one, each ding a step closer to their target.

When the elevator reached D'Anthony's floor, the doors slid open with a soft chime. Without hesitation, they stepped out, their footsteps echoing in unison as they speed-walked down the corridor. Their hearts pounded in their chests, adrenaline sharpening their focus. They approached the apartment, a singular purpose driving them forward.

***

D'Anthony and his friends were cleaning up the remnants of the previous night's party, laughing and joking, oblivious to the impending danger. The sound of crumpling cans and muffled conversations filled the room, masking the threat drawing near.

The door burst open with a thunderous crash, splintering wood and shattering their peace. Chyna, Bag Man, and Augustus stormed in, their rifles raised, the room falling into a stunned, terrified silence.

Ratatatatatatatatatatatatatat!

Ratatatatatatatatatatatatatat!

Chyna, Bag Man, and Augustus stood inside the living room with warm assault rifles. Once the gunsmoke cleared, they were standing before a holey couch, wall, and three ruined portraits. One of the portraits hanging crooked on the wall dropped and fell on the seat of the couch.

"Y'all check the bedrooms and the bathrooms. I'll cover the living room and the kitchen," Augustus gave the command and everyone disbursed.

Augustus flipped the couch, checked the closet, and searched every cabinet. By the time he'd finished, Bag Man and Chyna returned to the living room, shaking their heads.

"Fuck!" Augustus cursed, kicking over one of the chairs at the kitchen table.

"Yo, let's shake the spot before 9 comes," Chyna said, fleeing the apartment. Augustus and Bag Man were right on his heels.

***

Meanwhile

D'Anthony, gun held at his side, stared out of the peephole of Marlo's apartment door. Grant and Hill, guns held at their shoulders, were on either side of him.

Once Chyna and the gang cleared the line of vision of the peephole, D'Anthony turned to his soldiers, letting them know what the deal was.

"Them niggaz gon', son." D'Anthony tucked his piece at the small of his back.

"Well, come on, we can burn them down before they hop on the elevator." Hill grabbed the doorknob, ready to have niggaz' families making funeral arrangements.

"Bro, are you fuckin' stupid? All them shots don' woke the entire hood up," D'Anthony frowned. "We go after them fools now. There's gonna be a lotta gunplay, and then 12 is sure to come."

Hill looked at Grant to see if he was on his type of time, but he shook his head. "He's right, G. Besides, with the firepower them boys packin', these sticks we got gon' sho' have us face up in boxes."

Hill, after thinking about it for a moment, lowered his piece at his side. "A'ight. I'll kick my heels up for now, but we gotta see about gettin' at these niggaz, shorty. I'm not finna live the rest of my life lookin' over my shoulders. Them boys gotta go."

Hill sat his gun on the coffee table and re-lit the blunt he'd been smoking earlier. As he indulged, Grant plopped down on the couch beside him, and Hill passed the blunt to him.

D'Anthony walked to Marlo's bedroom to grab his cellphone. He needed to hit him up to let him know what was good. The way things were looking, D'Anthony was seriously considering grabbing the dough he'd buried back at the spot, and laying low in The Chi until he figured out how to handle Chyna and his gang without winding up dead, or locked up.

"Y'all get his ass?" Jayvon asked as Chyna, Bag Man, and Augustus walked through the door.

"Hell nah, bro," Chyna said regretfully, handing his assault rifle to Augustus, who also took Bag Man's weapon.

"What happened?" Chrissy asked, watching Augustus as he walked past her to put the firearms away, her face mirroring concern and frustration.

"Lil' muthafucka was gone before we got there," Bag Man chimed in, popping open a beer from the fridge and taking a long swig like it would drown his disappointment.

"Shit," Jayvon muttered, rubbing his temples in frustration. He'd been counting on them to deal with D'Anthony for pulling that fuck shit—stealing the stolen money right from under their noses. It was a slap in the face they couldn't afford to ignore.

"It's a'ight though," Chyna sighed heavily, sinking into the couch. "If he hasn't already skipped town, we're gonna eventually catch up with 'em."

Jayvon dropped down beside him. "You can't thinka anywhere else this kid might be?"

Chyna shook his head as he tried to piece together any missed clues. "Nah. Not right at this moment. That lil' bastard is slick, but he ain't invisible. Sooner or later, he's gonna slip up, and when he does, we gon' be right there to catch his ass."

CHAPTER THREE

The yellowing lightbulb dangling from the ceiling had the basement dimly lit. Liebowitz and Delroy were strapped back to back in chairs, surrounded by the same men who had stormed the grounds of Liebowitz's mansion. Half of the men had their AR-15s trained on the old man, while the other half stood by as Luka delivered a brutal beating. Luka's white dress shirt and fists were stained with blood, a stark contrast to the darkness of the room.

A final punch dislodged a broken tooth from Liebowitz's mouth. His chin dropped to his chest as he breathed jaggedly. LaDecia, who had been watching the assault the entire time, passed Luka a towel. He used it to dry the blood from his hands.

Luka leaned in close, his voice a low growl. "Are you ready to tell me where I can find my son now?"

Liebowitz spat blood onto Luka's shirt. "Kiss my rich, white ass," he snarled.

Luka smirked, a glint of respect in his eyes. "You've got testicles the size of bowling balls, I'll give you that." He held out his hand towards one of his henchmen, who pulled a pistol from his side holster, cocked it, and placed it in Luka's palm.

"It's a pity you couldn't be more cooperative," Luka said, pressing the gun to Liebowitz's forehead. LaDecia opened an umbrella, prepared to shield herself from the impending gore.

Just as Luka was about to pull the trigger, Delroy shouted, "Stop! I'll tell you who has your son, but I don't know where he is."

Liebowitz, his voice weak but defiant, urged, "Don't tell him shit, Delroy!"

Delroy glanced at Liebowitz, his eyes filled with sorrow. "I'm sorry, but I can't let him kill you."

Luka lowered the gun and his gaze shifted to Delroy. "Talk."

Delroy took a deep breath, his voice trembling. "I raised that kid from a pup. During his training, we grew a father-and-son bond. It pained me to watch him walk out of the mansion." A single tear slid down Delroy's cheek. "Our boy goes by the name Wild Child now, and a man named Bartise purchased him not long ago."

Luka gave a nod to one of his men, who stepped forward and cut Delroy free of his bindings. Once Delroy was loose, Luka faced him, his expression hard but resolute. "You'll be our guide in New York. You'll help us find our son, Neo—the name he was given at birth."

Delroy nodded, his spirit broken but his resolve firm. "I'll help you, but only if you promise to let Liebowitz go and ensure he gets medical attention."

Luka considered this for a moment before nodding. "Agreed." He turned to his henchmen. "See that the old man is taken care of."

LaDecia approached Delroy, her eyes assessing him critically. "If you're going to be our guide, we need to upgrade your attire. You will wear nothing short of the best while accompanying us."

Delroy nodded in agreement, his mind already shifting to the task ahead. He walked out of the basement with Luka and LaDecia, the weight of the mission pressing down on him but a glimmer of hope in his heart. Together, they would embark on a journey to find Neo.

***

After spending half the day shopping, Luka and LaDecia decided to treat Delroy to a meal at LaSalle's, a five-star Italian restaurant nestled in Little Italy. The ambiance was warm and inviting, with the aroma of freshly baked bread and rich marinara sauce wafting through the air. They settled into a private booth, and as they waited for their orders, Luka and LaDecia began to share their story.

"We escaped the clutches of our jailer, Demonte, with nothing but our lives and a few stolen bills," Luka began, his voice low and steady. "We turned that small fortune into half a billion dollars through smart investments in properties, businesses, and profitable ventures."

LaDecia nodded, adding, "We've been married for seventeen years, and during that time, we were imprisoned and forced to breed children in Demonte's incarceration camp. Thirteen children, to be exact."

Delroy listened intently, his eyes wide with shock and respect. "Thirteen children?" he repeated, incredulous.

"Yes," LaDecia confirmed. "We've managed to find seven of them so far. Once we catch up with Wild Child, he'll make eight. Our mission is to find all our children and reunite our family. Nothing will stand in our way."

As the waiters served their dishes—rich lasagna, creamy fettuccine alfredo, and a fresh Caprese salad—the conversation shifted to their current quest.

"Wild Child has always been special," Delroy said, a note of pride in his voice. "Like I said before, 'I raised him from a pup.

During his training, we developed a father-son bond. It pained me to see him walk out of the mansion.'"

Luka leaned in, his eyes sharp and focused. "We're grateful for everything you've done for him, Delroy. I'm positive it was your guidance that got our boy this far."

LaDecia reached across the table and grasped Delroy's hand. "We appreciate you so much. And we want to thank you properly."

After their meal, Luka pulled out his checkbook. "For your help in finding our son, we want to offer you this," he said, starting to write a check.

Delroy shook his head, a soft smile on his face. "I don't need your money, Luka. I want to do right by Wild Child. He's talked about finding his parents and reuniting with his family. That's payment enough for me."

Luka and LaDecia exchanged a look, their hearts swelling with gratitude and pride. "Thank you, Delroy," LaDecia said, her voice choked with emotion. "Knowing that our son wants to find us and be with us means more than anything in the world."

As they finished their meal and prepared to leave, the bond between them had grown stronger. They were united in their mission, driven by love and determination.

"This is just the beginning," Luka said as they stepped out into the bustling streets of Little Italy. "We have a long road ahead, but we'll find all our children and bring them home."

LaDecia nodded, squeezing his hand. "Together, we're unstoppable."

Delroy looked at them, a sense of purpose in his eyes. "I got y'all backs, every step of the way. That's my word."

CHAPTER FOUR

Delroy walked through the halls of the hospital with a mixed fruit arrangement in his hands. He found Liebowitz's room and gently pushed the door open. Inside, Liebowitz lay swollen and bandaged, with splints on his pinky and middle fingers. He looked up as Delroy entered, his face lighting up with a hint of a smile.

"Hey there, old man," Delroy greeted, setting the fruit arrangement on the push table beside the bed.

Liebowitz plucked a grape from the arrangement and popped it into his mouth. "Have you found Wild Child yet?" he asked, his voice rough but steady.

Delroy pulled a chair closer to Liebowitz's bedside and sat down. "That's why I'm here," he said. "I need your help. It would make things much easier if you gave me Bartise's contact info."

Liebowitz shook his head slowly. "I forgave you for giving up Wild Child's whereabouts out of love and respect, and the fact you saved my life. But I can't give you Bartise's number. It goes against my business practices. Besides," he added, tapping his temple, "I keep all my business associates' numbers up here."

Delroy sighed, shaking his head. "You're one stubborn old bastard, you know that?"

Liebowitz shrugged, a small smirk on his lips. "You don't get to live to be my age without flipping the bird to death."

Delroy leaned forward, his tone pleading. "Please, Liebowitz. Give me something that will lead me to Wild Child."

Liebowitz took a deep breath, thinking for a moment. "Alright," he said finally. "Grab my jacket out of the closet and get the golden envelope out of its right pocket."

Delroy quickly did as he was told, finding Bartise's golden fight tournament invitation inside the jacket pocket. He held it up, his eyes widening with hope.

"Bartise sent that invite to me," Liebowitz explained. "Wild Child will be competing there."

Delroy's face broke into a wide smile. "Thank you, Liebowitz. This means everything to us." He leaned over and hugged the old man gently. "I'll be back in a week to check on you."

As Delroy turned to leave, Liebowitz called out, "Good luck, Delroy. And bring our boy home."

Delroy ran into the hallway, clutching the golden envelope. His heart pounded with excitement as he dashed toward the elevator lobby, eager to share the news with Luka and LaDecia. As the elevator doors opened, he slipped inside, barely containing his excitement.

When the elevator reached the lobby, Delroy burst out, scanning the area for Luka and LaDecia. Spotting them near the entrance, he hurried over, waving the envelope in the air.

"I got it!" he shouted, a grin spreading across his face. "I know where Wild Child is going to be."

Luka and LaDecia's eyes widened with hope. "Where?" LaDecia asked, her voice trembling.

Delroy handed them the golden invitation. "Bartise's fight tournament. Wild Child will be there."

Luka and LaDecia exchanged a look of relief and determination. "We need to prepare," Luka said. "This is our chance to bring him home."

LaDecia nodded, her eyes shining with tears of joy. "Thank you, Delroy. You've given us hope."

As they left the hospital, the trio felt a renewed sense of purpose. The road ahead would be challenging, but they were ready to face it together. With the golden invitation in hand, they had a lead on Wild Child's whereabouts and a new mission to complete.

Delroy glanced at Luka and LaDecia, feeling a sense of unity and resolve. "We'll get him back," he said confidently. "No one will stand in our way."

***

It didn't dawn on Chyna until later that night where he may be able to find D'Anthony's ho-ass. He and the fellas didn't waste any time grabbing their guns among other things to see what was up. They found themselves at a house that wasn't much to look at, but Chyna knew it must have held some sort of sentimental value to D'Anthony. He recalled him saying if he needed somewhere to lay low or someplace to hide something, it would be at this place. Chyna never forgot where the house was located or what it looked like. The place was an ugly turquoise green. Its paint was chipped badly and it had amateur graffiti on its exterior.

"You sure this is the place, youngin'?" Bag Man asked.

"No doubt," Chyna replied.

"Well, let's get the tools and shit out so we can get to work," Augustus said. "Lil' homie may not be here, but maybe we can locate that money."

As the moon cast an eerie glow over the old, decrepit house, Chyna, Bag Man, and Augustus grabbed their pickaxes and LED work lights out of the hatch of their Lincoln Navigator. Moving stealthily, they slipped through the backdoor into the dark, musty kitchen.

They started hacking up the floor and the walls, the sound of splintering wood and crumbling plaster echoing through the silent house. When they didn't find the money, they moved to the living room, each man taking a wall. Still, no luck. Frustration mounting, they moved the work lights to the center of the floor.

Chyna raised his pickaxe above his head to strike the intended spot, but a flash of light and movement outside caught his eye. He signaled for Augustus to turn off the work lights and ducked to the floor, placing a finger to his lips for silence. The three men listened intently to the commotion outside.

Crawling over to one of the windows, Chyna stole a peek. He saw D'Anthony, Grant, and Hill walking alongside the house, shovels slung over their shoulders and flashlights guiding their way. Chyna crawled back to Bag Man and Augustus, whispering that D'Anthony and his crew were outside.

"Let's follow them into the kitchen and see what they're going to do," Chyna suggested.

CHAPTER FIVE

They crept into the kitchen, peeking out of the window over the sink. They watched as D'Anthony and his boys approached a tree with an X carved into its trunk. Grant shone the flashlight on an area D'Anthony pointed out, while he and Hill started digging.

"I bet they're digging up that money," Chyna whispered.

Augustus and Bag Man, guns drawn, whispered back that they should rob them once they dug up the loot. Chyna nodded, agreeing to wait until the work was done.

"Let them do the work for us," Bag Man added.

***

Once D'Anthony and his crew had unearthed the money, Chyna signaled for Augustus and Bag Man to follow him. They burst through the backdoor of the house, exchanging gunfire with D'Anthony and his boys. The air filled with the loud sound of gunshots and the smell of gunpowder. Augustus took a hit in his leg and thigh, gritting his teeth against the pain.

Grant and Hill frantically loaded the money into the backseat of their car while D'Anthony provided cover. Grant was cut down in the crossfire and he crumpled to the ground. D'Anthony and Hill dove into their car, bullets peppering the vehicle, leaving holes in the trunk and bumper.

***

As Chyna and Bag Man fired at the retreating car, Augustus, who had managed to sneak away, crashed the Navigator through the twin gates of the backyard. He swung open the backdoor and hollered for them to get in. D'Anthony sped away, tires screeching.

Chyna and Bag Man reloaded their guns and jumped into the backseat. Augustus floored the gas pedal before they could even close the door completely. Chyna crawled up to the passenger seat, urging Augustus not to lose them.

"Don't lose these muthafuckaz!" he shouted.

Bag Man rolled down his window and the cold night air rushed inside. They leaned out, ready to continue the shootout as they sped down the dark streets in pursuit of D'Anthony and Hill.

The Navigator roared through the streets, Augustus maneuvering like a professional getaway driver. They kept close to D'Anthony's car, which swerved wildly in a desperate attempt to shake them off.

D'Anthony tore through the streets, his Dodge Challenger roaring like a beast as it raced through the night. Augustus's Navigator was right on his ass, the tires screeching as they skidded around corners, the distance between them closing rapidly. The two vehicles were locked in a deadly pursuit, their speeds so intense that the world around them blurred into a streak of lights and shadows.

In the backseat of the Navigator, Chyna and Bag Man leaned out of the windows, their guns spitting fire as they exchanged bullets with Hill, who was hanging halfway out of the Challenger. The air was thick with the sound of gunfire, the sharp cracks echoing off the buildings around them. Bullet holes riddled both whips, and each shot sent shattered glass and shrapnel flying, creating a lethal rain that added to the chaos.

D'Anthony, his knuckles white as he gripped the steering wheel, made a sharp right turn, the tires screeching as he nearly lost control. The Challenger fishtailed, coming dangerously close to spinning out, but D'Anthony managed to regain control just in time. He swerved around a group of teenagers playing basketball in the street. As the vehicles raced through, the kids scrambled to get out of the way.

Bag Man and Chyna quickly ducked back inside the Navigator, ejecting the spent clips from their guns and slamming in fresh ones. As they did, Hill, now back inside the Challenger, did the same, his eyes narrowing as he glanced over his shoulder at the Navigator rapidly closing in on them.

***

"They're gaining on us!" Hill shouted, his voice dripping urgency.

D'Anthony didn't need to be told twice. His eyes flicked to the rearview mirror, catching sight of the Navigator inching closer with each passing second. The pressure was mounting, and he could feel the noose tightening around his neck.

Suddenly, the two vehicles erupted in gunfire again. Bag Man, Chyna, and Hill all reemerged from their respective windows, unleashing a barrage of bullets. The rapid exchange of gunfire was deafening. The vehicles weaved erratically as each man tried to avoid being hit.

Then, in a split second, everything changed. A stray bullet shattered the driver-side window of the Challenger, sending shards of glass into D'Anthony's face. He screamed in agony as the jagged shards pierced his eye and cheek, blood streaming down his face. His grip on the steering wheel faltered, and the car veered wildly off course, slamming into the back of an old brown Plymouth parked on the side of the road.

The impact was catastrophic. The windshield exploded as Hill was violently ejected from the car, his body flying through the air before crashing into the back window of the Plymouth. The glass cracked under the force, creating a spiderweb of fractures. Hill lay motionless, his face twisted into a grimace of death, blood pooling around him as most of the money from the Finesse lick spilled out of the car, fluttering through the air like fallen leaves.

D'Anthony, wincing in pain, pulled the glass shard from his eye and let it drop. He forced himself to look through the bloodied windshield. His heart sank when he saw Hill's lifeless body slumped against the Plymouth. It was a sight that filled him with horror and regret. "Damn, my nigga Hill," he muttered, knowing that his friend was gone.

But there was no time to mourn. The smell of gasoline filled the air as flames began to lick up from the crumpled hood of the Challenger, threatening to turn the wreck into an inferno. D'Anthony's instincts kicked in. He stuffed as much cash as he could into the pockets of his jacket before grabbing his Tec-9.

CHAPTER SIX

D'Anthony glanced over his shoulder and saw Chyna's car speeding toward him. He knew he had seconds, maybe less, to make his move. Crawling out of the passenger window, he dropped onto the sidewalk, wincing as pain shot through his injured leg. He forced himself to stand, limping away as fast as he could and taking cautious looks over his shoulder.

The Navigator skidded to a halt, and Chyna and Bag Man jumped out, eyes scanning the scene. They were surrounded by chaos as people from nearby houses and yards swarmed the street, grabbing fistfuls of cash that had spilled from the wreck. The duo was undeterred, their eyes laser-focused on finding D'Anthony.

"There that lil' shit go!" Bag Man shouted, pointing to where D'Anthony was limping away, trying to blend into the panicked crowd.

Without hesitation, they raised their weapons and opened fire. D'Anthony ducked and weaved through the crowd, bullets zipping past him as he sprinted toward the relative safety of a nearby house. He disappeared into the yard just as Chyna and Bag Man began to give chase.

But before they could catch up, the distant wail of sirens cut through the night air. Chyna and Bag Man skidded to a stop, their eyes locking onto the flashing lights of approaching police cars. They were coming in fast from two blocks away, their presence forcing a split-second decision.

"9!" Chyna shouted. "Fall back, now!"

Bag Man hesitated, his frustration boiling over, but he knew there was no time to argue. With one last look in the direction D'Anthony had fled, he turned and followed Chyna back to the Navigator. They jumped in, and Augustus floored the gas pedal, the tires screeching as they sped away from the scene, leaving behind the wreckage, the money, and the chaos.

Augustus adjusted his rearview mirror just in time to see D'Anthony's car explode. The deafening blast was followed by a chorus of panicked screams as people darted back and forth across the street, burning money raining down. Flames danced in the reflection, casting an eerie glow on the bedlam.

Chyna and Bag Man sat in tense silence, their minds already racing ahead to what came next. D'Anthony had slipped through their fingers, but the chase would come to a close soon.

***

Trick had taken the beating of a lifetime, but through the grace of God, he was still alive. The hospital at the prison didn't have everything they needed to treat him, so he had to be airlifted to a suitable medical facility. He suffered a concussion, a broken eye socket, fractured cheekbones, and a metal plate was made to replace part of his skull. His left arm and right leg were in a cast. With all the trauma he'd been through the doctors were surprised he was still breathing. They believed a lesser man would have undoubtedly met his end.

Though Trick was in a coma, his mind sparked with electrical currents of activity. He began experiencing everything that landed him in prison and his current predicament. Everyone that entered his room didn't notice but his eyelids and fingers would twitch, as if they were reanimating.

Trick vowed to pay Apryl and Dario back for destroying his family. He could handle them breaking his heart but breaking the hearts of his children was something he couldn't let slide. So here he was, a few months later, with murder on his mind.

***

I already handled that fuck-nigga Dario back on his private jet. Now it's time I get at Apryl. Punk bitch gon' leave me and our boys for this wetback Cuban mothafucka, and think she's gon' live happily ever after? Shawty you got me fucked up on all levels. Musta forgot I'ma straight-up goon out here in these streets. I'ma make you, him and them bitchez runnin' unda him put some respect on my name, Trick thought. His face twisted in hatred and he gritted his teeth. He gripped the steering wheel so tight his knuckles cracked. He was so close to settling his beef with his trifling-ass wife and his ex-boss that he could taste it on the tip of his tongue.

Trick adjusted the earbud in his ear and passed one to Jayvon who did the same. He turned down the radio to check and see if the earbuds worked properly.

"Testin', testin', one, two, three..." Trick said loud enough for Jayvon to hear him. "You hear me comin' through on yo' end?"

"I hear you, Pop." Jayvon nodded.

"Good," Trick replied, making a right at the corner.

"Pop, do you have one for me to try?" Chyna asked, leaning in between the two front seats.

"Baby boy, this here, ain't a toy."

"I know it's notta toy, Pop. I just wanna see how it works. Please, please, please." Chyna begged with his hands together.

Trick thought it over as he drove down the street. His youngest son wasn't your typical ten-year-old. He was mature for his age and carried himself like someone three times his age. He'd shown the boy how to fight, handle a gun, a hatchet, and a hunting knife, and even taught him how to drive. He figured letting him fool around with the earbud wasn't a big deal compared to him handling more serious objects.

"Awight, baby boy." Trick said, removing the earbud and passing it to Chyna. Excited, Chyna hugged him with one arm and kissed him on the cheek, which made him smirk.

"Big bruh, can you hear me?" Chyna asked as he sat back in the seat.

"Yeah, I can hear you, lil' bruh. What's goodie?"

"Nothing much. I think this is gonna be the best night ever."

Trick looked up at Chyna through the rearview mirror. He felt like a piece of shit for having lied to his boy but he viewed it as a necessary evil. He'd told them they were going to break into Dario's mansion and rescue their mother to bring her back home. Although Apryl had left on her own merit, he'd spun a story about Dario holding her hostage in his mansion and refusing to let her leave. The truth was Trick planned on breaking into the mansion and blowing their mother away. There was no way he was going to get back with that bitch. She'd left her family to run off with a nigga.

Trick listened to his sons' conversation over the earbuds as he drove. He hated to have to bring them along on this mission because no matter how he looked at it his sons were undoubtedly helping him kill their mother. If they were to ever find out about what he'd involved them in he wasn't sure if they could ever forgive him. Trick wanted to bring along the niggaz that he fucked with Hardbody but they didn't want any parts of his deathly situation. All that meant to him was they were scared of their boss which was why he killed them—all three of them. Sure it may sound fucked up but he couldn't risk them reporting to Dario what he planned to do to him. As far as he was concerned the moment those fools declined to ride on the drug lord with him they chose whose side they were on.

Trick parked far from Dario's mansion where his Chevrolet couldn't be seen. The moment he put the car in park his cellphone chimed with a text message. He pulled it out of his pocket and checked it. It was the stewardess onboard Dario's private jet that he'd dropped a bag on. She and her boyfriend, who was the pilot of the aircraft, mission to poison Dario and his security team with cyanide.

Trick smiled as he looked down at his cellular. The text message the stewardess sent him confirmed that the deed was done. He then gave her the address to the train station, the locker number as well as the combination to the lock where the other half of the money for the mission was located.

"Pop, what're you smiling about?" Chyna asked.

"Yeah, Pop, I haven't seen you smile like that inna while. What's up?" Jayvon added.

"Boy, I got two nosy ass sons." Trick grinned, pocketing his cellular. He then switched seats with Jayvon so he'd be in the driver's seat. "Awight, I'll be right back, Jayvon, keep her runnin'." Trick pulled a ski mask over his face. He hugged and kissed Jayvon. Then he hugged and kissed Chyna. "I love y'all, both of y'all."

"We love you too, Pop," Jayvon replied.

"Yeah, me the most." Chyna leaned over into the front seat.

Trick smiled and ruffled Chyna's head. "If I'm not back in twenty minutes, y'all get the hell outta here. Ya hear me, Scrap?" Jayvon nodded understandingly. "Smooth."

Trick pulled out his black .45 semi-automatic pistol and screwed a metallic gray silencer on its barrel. He gently closed the passenger door when he stepped out of the box Chevrolet. He tucked his heat at the small of his back and made hurried footsteps toward the mansion.

CHAPTER SEVEN

Jayvon and Chyna watched as the night swallowed their father like a humpback whale.

"You think Pop is gonna come back with ma?" Chyna asked.

"I don't know," Jayvon said, taking in his surroundings as he drummed his fingers on the steering wheel.

"Well, I hope so. Then we can be a family again." Chyna sat back in his seat, staring out of the back window.

***

Trick paid an inside man a pretty penny to make the security alarms useless and loop the surveillance cameras. In addition to that, he stole Dario's keys and made duplicates of them. The plan was for the inside man to act like he had a family emergency so he could leave early. Once he'd gone, Trick would sneak on the grounds of the estate, euthanize the guards, and eliminate his two-timing wife once and for all.

Trick glanced at his digital timepiece. It was 10:45 p.m. His inside man was to give his colleagues his bullshit excuse at 10:40 p.m. so he should have been leaving now. Trick crept alongside the mansion, occasionally hiding inside the bushes to see if anyone was watching him. Making it to the front, he peered around the corner to see a white Cadillac Seville CT5 driving out of the black gates.

That's Gil's fat-ass car. It's time I make my move, Trick thought as he licked his shiny gold teeth. He took a mental note of all the armed guards standing out front. They were oblivious to his presence which was exactly like he wanted it. He searched the grounds until he found a rock, tossing it up and down in his hand. He threw it high and long across the air and it deflected off the side of the mansion, stealing the guard's attention.

"What the hell was that?" He said to no one in particular. He frowned as he gripped his assault rifle and crept towards the sound he'd heard. "Yo', Eduardo, you hear that?"

"I didn't hear shit, Miguel! Now shut up talking to me while my dick is in my hand, I'm tryna take a piss." Eduardo said from over his shoulder, somewhere on the other side of the mansion.

Miguel, who'd heard the sound, crept toward a bush and used his assault rifle to sift through it. Hearing soft footfalls at his back, he turned around to spray whoever was coming at him and got the surprise of a lifetime. Trick upped his piece and sent a silent bullet right through his throat. A pained expression came across Miguel's face and blood spurted out the hole in his neck. Trick caught him before he could hit the ground and drug him back somewhere around the mansion. He stashed him between the bushes and made his rounds around the estate. He moved as stealthy and as swift as a C.I.A. trained assassin. First, he took out Eduardo then he moved to the guards posted at the double doors of the mansion. He gave them niggaz chest shots. They dropped their assault rifles and tumbled down the stairs.

Trick scanned the area to make sure there weren't any more guards on the premises. Gilbert told him there would be a total of six of them including himself so there were only two more left. He figured they'd be somewhere inside of the mansion, possibly holding Apryl down, if not fucking her ho-ass.

Trick kneeled to check the pulse in the guards' necks he'd blasted. Once he confirmed their deaths, he made his way up the stairs pulling out the copy of the keys Gilbert had made for him. Unlocking the door, he snuck inside and closed the door as gently as he could. Unfortunately, he wound up closing the door too hard and it made a click loud enough for anyone within earshot to hear.

Trick made sure the lower level of the mansion was clear before going onto the upper level. He closed his eyes for a moment, visualizing the map Gilbert had drawn for him so he'd recall where the master bedroom was located. He opened his eyes once he'd made it to the second floor. Keeping his gun low, he snuck down a hallway that looked like it would never end. He could hear Nina Simone's "Don't Let Me Be Misunderstood" playing. That was Apryl's favorite song. She was an old record collector so he brought her the vinyl for their third wedding anniversary.

Yeah, I know yo' ass up here now, bitch. Ain't none of dem Cuban niggaz gon' be listenin' to no Nina, Trick smiled wickedly behind his ski mask, thinking how sweet it was going to be to blow his wife's pretty little head off. The record continued to play as he crept down the hallway. He was sweating profusely underneath his mask so he decided to take it off and tuck it inside of his right back pocket. It didn't matter who saw his face now because he wasn't leaving until he'd flatlined every living soul in that bitch!

Trick gently twisted the knob and opened the door. When he stepped inside he found Apryl standing out on the terrace. She was dressed in a red silk robe, bra, and panties. Her head was tilted back and her eyes were closed. She wore a smile on her lips as the wind blew into her face and made her long, curly hair drift behind her. Feeling an aura behind her, Apryl's eyes popped open and she lowered her head. She didn't have to turn around to know who was creeping up behind her. She knew it was her husband and kids' father.

"Trick," Apryl spoke the intruder's name and pressed the panic button that was the ruby at the center of the cross hanging from her gold necklace. The panic button would alert the guards inside the mansion to the presence of danger and they'd come running to her aid.

"You thought chu was gon' getta way from me, didn't chu, shawty?" Trick crossed the threshold, swinging his gun around in different directions. He expected the last two guards to be lurking somewhere inside the master bedroom but they weren't there. "You coulda dug a hole halfway to China to hide yo' thot-ass in and I woulda found you eventually. You played me and our boys for some foreign, swingin' dick! Well, I hope you're happy, 'cause yo' betrayal costa lotta folks their lives! That fuck-nigga Dario, and several of those goons he has posted up around this place."

Apryl closed her eyes and bowed her head. Clutching the platinum cross in her hand, she recited a prayer just above a whisper, hoping Dario's men would come bursting into the bedroom to save her. Right then, two of Dario's goons rushed inside the bedroom and drew down on Trick.

"Drop it puto, or we'll blow that gold grill outta your fuckin' mouth!" The goon threatened, cocking back the hammer of his gun.

"Suck whatta got hangin' low!" Trick snarled. He didn't bother turning around. His eyes and his .45 were pinned on Apryl.

"Fuck it! Let's drop this pinche pendejo!" the other goon said, cocking back the hammer of his gun.

The goons opened fire on Trick and bullets ripped through the fabric of his clothing. He clenched his teeth to combat the pain and started busting at Apryl. Two hot ones zipped through her chest and her face balled up. She was about to fall forward when a third bullet blew a nickel-sized hole through her forehead. The impact flipped her over the handrail and she plummeted fifteen-feet toward the swimming pool below.

Trick collided with the floor with his arm tucked under him. It was about ten holes in his black jacket from the goons clapping him. The goons, with their guns pinned on Trick, walked towards him cautiously. He lay where he was still and stiff.

"You think he's dead?" one goon asked the other.

"With as many bullets as we pumped into him, I'd say, yes." the other goon replied.

"I'll check him out, you see what's up with her."

"Are you kidding me? He shot her three times. One of those was in the head." the second goon said, holding his shoulder holster and shoving his piece inside of it.

"You never know." The first goon replied, switching hands with his pistol and kneeling to Trick. He turned him over to check his pulse and his eyes suddenly popped open. Trick pulled the trigger of his banger, twice. The first bullet struck the goon below *his left eye and the second right between his eyes. He killed over, falling on top of Trick.*

CHAPTER EIGHT

The second goon, who was on his way out onto the terrace, turned around grabbing for his holstered gun. He'd drawn it halfway when Trick outstretched his gun from where he lay trapped underneath his colleague. He squeezed off three times and as many empty shell casings jumped out of his pistol. The goon grimaced and dropped to his knees. He'd taken one in his stomach and two in his chest. His eyes rolled to their whites and he fell on his face.

A wincing Trick pushed the goon that had fallen on him over onto the floor and got upon his feet. He lifted his holey shirt, revealing a white bulletproof vest, covered in dents from his being shot.

"Arrrrg," Trick grumbled painfully. His body armor may have stopped him from being killed, but the impact of the bullets still hurt like hell. Trick took the time to reload his banger before stepping out onto the terrace. When he looked over the handrail he saw Apryl sinking into the pool's diluted water while her brain fragments floated around her. Police sirens drew Trick's attention to the gates of the mansion. Several police cars spilled onto the grounds of the estate, heading his way.

"Oh, shit!" Trick said under his breath. "Outta the fryin' pan and into the fuckin' fire."

"Pop, are you good? I heard mad shots up there!" Jayvon came in over the earbud.

"I'm okay, Scrap, finna be on my way so keep Yolanda runnin'." Trick spoke of his Box Chevy. "The Johnnies rollin' thick ass shit."

"I gotchu, pop."

"Awight. I'm out." Trick replied. He ran back as far as he could in the master bedroom. He got down in a runner's position, looking like he was waiting for a starter pistol to be fired. Abruptly, he took off running, passing up the dead bodies on the bedroom floor, hearing a helicopter overhead, coming in his direction.

Trick crossed the threshold out onto the terrace, pushed off the handrail, and leaped high into the air. As he plummeted towards the pool he flailed his arms and kicked his legs. Trick broke the surface of the pool's water and made a big splash. The police helicopter's spotlight shone down on him through the murky water. Bubbles manifested out of his nose as he swam across the pool. He came across Apryl's dead body as it was sinking to the bottom but he didn't pay it any mind.

As soon as Trick pulled himself out of the pool, he was ducking and dodging gunfire from the Johnnies. He reached for his gun that he'd tucked at the small of his back but it wasn't there. His brows wrinkled with confusion, wondering where the hell he'd lost it. That's when he saw it on the floor of the pool. He figured it must have slipped out of his waistband when he splashed into the water. Just then, the police helicopter's spotlight shone on him again. He stole a glance up at it but the oncoming gunfire from the Johnnies reminded him he was in a deadly situation.

Trick hauled ass with the Johnnies and the spotlight followed him like they had a vendetta. He ducked and zig zagged, to avoid the line of gunfire coming at him.

"Haa! Haa! Haa! Haa! Haa!" Trick huffed and puffed as he ran. He occasionally glanced over his shoulders to see how far behind the cops were. The gap between them was large enough for him to possibly get away but that goddamn helicopter was on him like white girls on NBA players.

"Pop! Pop! What's going on, man? I heard gunshots!" Jayvon came over the earbud again.

"This is the police, lay down on your stomach, and place your hands behind your head!" a commanding voice spoke through the megaphone.

Trick threw the middle finger up at the helicopter and continued his sprint. When he heard barking over his shoulders, he looked back and three German Shepherds were chasing him. They looked like they couldn't wait to tear him apart.

Goddamn, bruh, they wanta nigga head, Trick thought.

"Pop! Pop! Are you okay? Tell me somethin', please!" A worried Jayvon asked, voice cracking emotionally.

"Take your brotha and get the hell outta here, now!" Trick finally replied.

"Man, fuck this, I'm comin' Pop, I'm comin' right now!" Jayvon told him.

"No, Scrap, don't come! Get outta here, get out!" Trick said, holding his finger against his earbud. "Shiiiiiit!"

***

"Ugh," Trick grumbled, landing on his bending knees after scaling the fence. He could still hear the helicopter and K-9s, but he was determined to get away. Breathing heavily, he wiped the sweat sliding down his forehead, looking around for someplace to run. He took off running south but the overwhelming surge of police cars sent him retreating in the opposite direction. He slid to a stop seeing another surge of police cars coming at him. The helicopter's spotlight shone on him as he turned around in a 360-degree circle, looking for another escape route.

Trick, realizing he was trapped, placed his hands behind his head and got down on his knees. Although he wasn't even close to dying, his life flashed before his eyes. The good times and the bad times! Those memories were all he'd have to keep him going because he was going to spend the rest of his life behind bars.

The cops drew down on Trick, with one of them barking orders at him. They may as well have been talking through soundproof glass because he couldn't hear them. Trick was laser-focused on Jayvon who was lying in the cut with his gun at his side. He could tell by the look in his eyes was ready to pull some kamikaze shit to save him but he couldn't allow that to happen. He loved his boys with all that he was and if he was to lose either one of them he'd go insane.

Trick shook his head, no. Jayvon frowned and his eyes misted. It was killing him not to come out from hiding and lay some of those pigs down. But he understood his old man's reasoning for wanting him to stand down. The cops would chop him down with extreme prejudice before he reached his father.

Jayvon sighed regretfully and his shoulders dropped. As soon as he tucked his piece at the small of his back, Chyna ran out from behind him teary-eyed, heading for their father. Jayvon snatched him back into him and covered his mouth. Chyna tried his best to *break free of his brother's hold but he was too strong. After a while he went limp in his brother's arms, sobbing long and hard.*

Trick stared at his boys with tears streaming down his cheeks as the cops handcuffed him. His heart split in two and he swallowed a lump of hurt. The cops pulled him up roughly to his feet and escorted him away. He looked over his shoulder, to see his boys crying and watching him being taken away. He mouthed "I love you" to them and they mouthed it back. The cops deposited him into the backseat of one of their cars. He looked out the back window and his boys had vanished. It was as if they were never there in the first place.

Trick knew his actions would most likely lead to an early grave or life in prison, so he made peace with that the moment he picked up his gun. The only thing that got to him was being away from his children. He was so blinded by getting even he didn't consider what would happen to his kids should he be caught. Since he was incarcerated he didn't know whether his kids were okay or not. He spent most of his time exercising, reading, and thinking about them. He didn't dare reach out to the authorities, so they could check in on them. He feared if he did his boys would be placed into the system, where they'd be beaten, molested, and raped. Trick didn't want that for his boys. Though they were tough they were still kids.

Still, his not being able to contact them while he was locked up was driving him mad. He could only think of the worst happening to them while in the streets alone.

Determined to get back on the streets to ensure his family was okay, Trick began brainstorming ways to escape from prison alongside four other convicts. There was a 50/50 chance they wouldn't make it from behind the wall but Trick was willing to risk it.

When the day of the prison break arrived, Trick got an anonymous letter from someone. He was anxious to see who had written him since he had little to no contact with the family he did have back South. He tore the letter open and looked over it. His eyes became misty as he read the letter. It was someone who'd been in recent contact with his boys. They were letting him know they were in good hands and being well taken care of. Tears burst from his eyes and rolled down his cheeks. When he got down to the bottom of the letter and it was signed, Love, the boys, Scrap & Mighty Mouse, his emotions got the best of him. These were the nicknames he'd given to Jayvon and Chyna. Jayvon had gotten his on the account he was always fighting and Chyna got his because he was a runt but was still with the shits.

"Oh, thank you, thank you, thank you, Gawd!" Trick said joyfully, dropping down on his knees and looking up at the ceiling. He bowed down to the floor, continuously giving praise to a

Higher Power. "Thank you for keepin' my babies safe since I've been down."

Trick calmed down and wiped away his tears. He kissed the cement floor as if it were the feet of Christ, thanked him again, and then laid back on his bunk. He kissed the letter he'd received and closed his eyes. He drifted off to sleep with a grin on his lips and his children on his mind.

CHAPTER NINE

Trick woke up yawning and stretching his arms and legs. He sat up on his bunk and looked to the floor. There was a kite at the corner of the bars of his cell. Omari, homie in the cell next to his, was most likely hitting him up about the prison break. Trick picked up the kite and sure enough, Omari was asking if he was still down with the move. Trick thought about it for a minute, and decided to fall back. He shot a kite back to Omari letting him know where he stood regarding the prison break.

"Say, Trick, you sho' 'bout dat, big dawg?" Omari asked in his South Central, Los Angeles accent. He was standing at his cell with his arms hanging out from between the bars.

"Yeah, bruh, I'm sho', don't worry though, gangsta. I'ma hold it down." Trick replied, meaning he wouldn't say a word about their escape attempt.

"No doubt, loved one, that's why I fucks witchu," Omari replied, tapping his fist against his chest. He stepped away from the bars and prepared for the night's move.

Trick sat back down on his bunk and read the letter Jayvon had sent him over and over again. He read it so much that he could actually see his oldest son and hear him talking to him. He resumed his regular program for the rest of the day.

A couple of days later, while Trick was reading, he got word from a convict mopping the floor by his cell that Omari and the other cons had been killed during the escape.

"Yeah, maine, dat redneck cracka Brewster dat they keep up there in that tower, spotted them makin' a run foe it and chopped dem boys down," the baldhead convict said as he mopped the floor.

"That's wild, bruh. O and 'nem was some good niggaz. I hate to hear that 'bout them boys." Trick shook his head sadly. He had mad love for Omari and the rest of the guys. So hearing they were gunned down had him in his feelings.

"Well, lemme get outta here foe this punk-ass C.O. come back around here pitchin' a fit." the convict told him, mopping back the way he'd come.

"To think, I almost made that move wit them boys," Trick shook his head again as he closed his book, setting it aside. He *couldn't help thinking he had one more thing to thank the Man Above for.*

Later that night the lights were turned off inside of Trick's cell. He laid back on his bunk and interlocked his fingers behind his head. He stared at the ceiling wondering what would become of his boys in his absence.

***

Berrios loomed over Trick as he lay in bed, wondering if he had it in him to take his life should the time ever come. Hands together in prayer, Berrios looked at the ceiling.

"God. I beg of you. Please, don't put me in a situation where I may have to break one of your commandments. Please," he took a breath and then walked out of the room.

***

Augustus's face was contorted in pain when Chyna and Bag Man brought him through the door of Jayvon's mansion. They carefully propped his wounded leg up at the dining room table, and Chrissy quickly moved into action, tying two of her scarves around his leg to slow the bleeding. Her fingers flew over her phone as she looked up how to remove a bullet from the dark web. With the necessary items gathered, she donned latex gloves and watched the video intently as she proceeded to remove the first bullet.

Jayvon passed Augustus a bottle of expensive whiskey. "Here. This should help with the pain."

Augustus took a long swig, wincing as Chrissy worked. Chyna recounted the events at the decrepit house, his voice filled with frustration and regret. "Man, we were so close. They dug up the money, but it slipped through our fingers."

Angry, Jayvon slammed his fist into his palm. "Damn. All that dough is gone. Might as well have started up a furnace and tossed every dollar in there."

Chyna hung his head. "My bad, bro. I fucked up."

Jayvon shook his head. "Don't sweat it. We still have the tournament as a source to get the loot we need."

Bag Man nodded. "Indeed we do. You and I are gonna start your training first thing tomorrow morning."

Chrissy gave Jayvon a worried look. She didn't want him risking his life in the tournament, but Jayvon waved off her concern. "Fa sho," he replied, determination hardening his voice.

Once Chrissy removed the bullets and dressed Augustus's wounds, Jayvon leaned in. "I need you to stay behind and watch over Chrissy when we fly to Bali for the tournament."

Augustus nodded and they dapped up, sealing the agreement.

Bag Man peered out the window. "Yo, there's some broad at the gate. Cute too."

Chyna and Jayvon crowded the window, looking over Bag Man's shoulder. They saw a young Black woman with long purple hair, dreamy eyes, thick, juicy lips, and a body that looked sculpted by the hands of God's most trusted angels.

Jayvon held down a button on the wall to speak to the visitor at the gate. "Yo, whaddup, shorty?"

She replied, "Hey, my name's Akita. I'm here on behalf of King Morpheus. He sent me to drop a package off to King Chyna."

Chyna's eyes lit up with recognition. "Yo, bro, let her in," he told Jayvon.

Jayvon shook his head. "Hell nah, baby boy. Go holler at lil' mama at the gate. She ain't setting foot in my crib. I should clothesline yo' lil' ass for dropping her my addy in the first place," he said, playfully punching Chyna's shoulder.

"I didn't give her the address, nigga," Chyna retorted. "King Morpheus must've dug it up somehow." He tucked his gun as he opened the front door.

"Unc, flank this lil' nigga and make sho' he's good," Jayvon instructed Bag Man.

Bag Man nodded, grabbing his gun and following Chyna out the door. "Hold up," he called, catching up to Chyna as they walked toward the gate.

Chyna and Bag Man approached Akita at the gate. Chyna introduced himself and Bag Man, keeping his tone friendly but professional.

"Nice to meet chu, Bag Man," Akita said with a smile, her eyes lingering on his stoic face.

Bag Man nodded curtly. "That's what's up."

Despite her friendly demeanor, Bag Man remained reserved. He always disliked bringing new talent into the fold because it meant a smaller slice of the pie for him. Akita, unfazed, handed a designer knapsack through the bars of the gate.

"Here you go," she said.

Chyna took the knapsack and peeked inside. His eyes widened in surprise at the sight of stacks of money and a box containing the latest iPhone.

"Thanks, Akita," Chyna said, genuine gratitude in his voice.

She nodded, turning to leave. "Take care, Chyna. Good luck with everything."

***

The gang gathered around the dining room table. Jayvon, Bag Man, Chrissy, and Augustus watched as Chyna set the knapsack on the table and began pulling out its contents. The stacks of money, the gun, and the iPhone box were laid out before them.

"Damn, that's a lot of cash," Jayvon said, a hint of excitement in his voice.

Chyna nodded, his focus shifting to the iPhone box. "Let's see what else we got here."

He opened the box and took out the sleek new iPhone. Turning it on, he waited for it to power up, the anticipation palpable in the room. The screen lit up, displaying a welcome message. Then the iPhone rang with the name "KING". The room fell silent, all eyes on Chyna as he contemplated his next move. He answered the call, his voice steady but cautious.

"What up, King?"

"I see shorty got that to you," King Morpheus's voice came through, calm but authoritative.

"Yeah. She just left, not long ago," Chyna replied.

"Like I said back at the burial, you're gonna be running the show from out there. Me and mine got it in here. Lil' mama toss you them bandz, too?"

Chyna confirmed, "Got that too, big homie. You know me and gang found out who the hittaz was."

"Nigga, who?" Morpheus asked anxiously.

"D'King," Chyna revealed. "You bumped into 'em at bro's funeral. He and Bocka clicked up for what we stole and left us holding our dicks. We tried finding them, but they got Swayze. A few days later, we find out Dolph and Chunky were left dead in the spot and Bocka got his wig puffed out."

The gravity of Chyna's words hung in the air. The gang exchanged glances, each absorbing the implications of the revelation. King Morpheus's silence on the other end of the line spoke volumes.

"If that's the case then the lil' nigga gotta get dealt wit," Morpheus finally said in a thoughtful tone.

Chyna wanted to be the one to knock D'Anthony down himself, but just in case he couldn't, he made sure to inform King Morpheus of everything he'd uncovered. He didn't hold back, detailing how the young nigga was the mastermind behind robbing him and his crew of the fortune they'd juxed Finesse for, then murdered Dolph and Bocka so he could keep the money for himself, how it all stemmed from greed and a thirst for power.

King Morpheus listened in cold silence, absorbing every detail. When Chyna finished, there was a pause, the kind that made the air feel thick.

"Breaking the rules to save your old man...I ain't sweating that," King Morpheus finally said, his tone even, but with an underlying edge that could cut steel. "But next time come to me first if you ever face some shit like that again. You understand?"

Chyna nodded, knowing the weight of that promise. "Yeah, King. I got chu."

"As far as our mutual friend goes, I'll put some of my knights on 'em," King Morpheus continued, voice low and ominous, "If

I'm that lil' muthafucka, I'd be tryna get on the first flight outta the city."

"Me, too."

"I'll get up witchu inna few days to properly welcome you into the fold, King. One hunnit."

"One."

King Morpheus hung up the call, leaving Chyna staring at the screen of his cellphone. The finality of the conversation settled over him like a dust cloud. He knew then—D'Anthony was living on borrowed time.

CHAPTER TEN

Meanwhile D'Anthony, gritting his teeth against the pain, hopped the back gate of a nearby house, narrowly avoiding a barking German Shepherd straining at its leash. He vaulted over the backyard fence, landing hard but steadying himself as he hurried down the driveway.

He stumbled to a stop, his breath coming in ragged gasps. D'Anthony opened his jacket and looked down at his gut. Two nickel-sized bullet holes stared back at him, the lower half of his shirt soaked in blood. "Goddammit," he cursed, his voice a raw whisper. Leaning against the side of the house, he stripped down to his wife-beater and tore it into strips. His hands shook as he tied the makeshift bandages around his wounds, snugly enough to slow the bleeding.

Slipping his jacket back on, he wandered off the residential block, his vision blurring at the edges. He reached an intersection and paused, seeing a cab idling across the street. With a sharp whistle, he waved a blood-stained handful of hundred-dollar bills at the driver. The light turned green, and the cab sped over, the driver's eyes widening at the sight of the cash.

"Get me to the LAX, and all that's yours," D'Anthony ordered, tossing the soiled bills through the passenger window.

The driver snatched the money and nodded eagerly. "You got it, buddy."

D'Anthony slid into the backseat, his body slumping against the worn upholstery. The cab peeled away from the curb, the engine's hum contrasting to the chaos he'd left behind. D'Anthony's skin had turned a ghostly pale, sweat beading on his forehead. He glanced down at the bloody strips around his torso, grimacing as he felt the life ebbing out of him.

He was starting to feel woozy, his eyelids growing heavy. Desperate to stay conscious, he pulled a small vial from his pocket and snorted a line of coke off his fist. The sudden jolt of the drug sent a fiery rush through his veins, momentarily sharpening his senses. The cab driver saw him through the rearview mirror but kept his mouth shut. He didn't want to jeopardize the windfall of at least three grand sitting in the passenger seat.

As they sped through the night, D'Anthony fought to keep his eyes open, the world outside blurring into a kaleidoscope of lights and shadows. He had one goal: to make it to LAX. The pain, the blood, the danger—all of it would be worth it if he could just get on a plane and disappear.

The cab driver kept glancing at him nervously, but D'Anthony didn't care. All he could think about was getting out, escaping the nightmare he'd found himself in. The coke flooding his system was a temporary fix to a permanent problem but he welcomed its effects. He could feel his strength waning, but he clung to consciousness, determined to see this through.

D'Anthony's mind drifted to better times and a grin tugged at the corners of his lips.

***

Chyna sat low in what he liked to call his jack mobile. He wore a black Raiders cap pulled just above his brows, $5 sunglasses, and a black bandana around his neck, cowboy style. Chyna peered through the tinted passenger window alongside his prospect, D'Anthony. The youngin' licked his lips as he stroked the Draco in his lap like it was a Persian cat.

"There them niggaz go right there, son." D'Anthony told Chyna. The little homie and his mentor watched as two men emerged from a housing complex and made their way across the parking lot. They were wearing icy platinum chokers, Rolexes,

and designer clothes. Chyna and D'Anthony knew they were papered up. It wasn't necessarily the jewels or the expensive drip, but the way they were carrying on like they didn't have a care in the world. The niggaz Chyna and D'Anthony knew coming up in the hood never behaved in such a manner. They were too busy scheming on a come-up so they could get the fuck out of the ghetto. These guys right here didn't have that to worry about. This was made clear when one of them had the nerve to pull out his cellphone, to make a call while the other busied himself doing God knew what on his. When they should have been looking out for Jack Kings, like Chyna and D'Anthony.

These are some dumb ass niggaz, bro. They're not even paying attention to what the fuck is going on, D'Anthony thought, shaking his head at how the hustlers were slipping. He didn't know it but Chyna was thinking the same thing.

Chyna nudged him and said, "Gone slide on yo' mask so you can hop out and do yo' shit."

box and removed the purple ski mask. He pulled it over his face and fixed its eye holes so he could see out of it. He held his Draco in one hand and used the other to open the back door. As soon as the Nissan came up the block past him, he hopped out of the truck and shut the door quietly. Hunching down low, and gripping his stick with both hands, he hurried around the big body SUV, coming up on the carriers fast. By the time they saw him, it was too late for them to reach for their gun so they threw their hands up.

"Drop the bag, and kick that shit over!" D'Anthony ordered, pointing the deadly end of his Draco at the hustlers.

"Look, homie, I gotta 'bout five bands on me, you can have that. But I can't give you this bag, 'cause if I don't see my boss with this, I'ma dead man. You feel me?" The lanky baldhead hustler told him. He looked like he'd rather take a bullet than come up off that duffle bag.

D'Anthony angled his head to the side and narrowed his eyes, looking at him like he was a special kind of stupid. He then shot him in the thigh, dropping him to the ground. Homie landed on his ass, clutching his bleeding leg and hollering.

"Nigga, you think I give a mad ass fuck 'bout cho problems? Huh? Now, I want all y'all shit, even them jewels y'all got on. Break mine off; I need all that shit, on gang!" D'Anthony demanded that the other goon open the duffle bag and fill it with whatever cash and jewelry they had on them. "Y'all guns, too! Those Italian leather loafers look 'bout my size, gemme them shits." The other man took the sticks from him and his partner's waistbands. He placed them into the duffle bag. He then placed him and his homeboy's loafers inside the bag. He zipped the duffle bag up, and while mad dogging D'Anthony, he tossed the bag over to him. D'Anthony grabbed the duffle bag and hoisted it over his shoulder. He locked eyes with the man and noticed he was pissed off. The nigga'z eyes were filled with hatred and his jaws were clenched so tight they pulsated. "Yo, son, I'm feeling mad heat comin' off you, you got somethin' you wanna get off yo' chest, my guy?"

The man squeezed his eyes shut and took a deep breath. When he peeled his eyes open again, the hostility seemed to have vanished from his face.

"Nah, it's all good." The man lied smoothly. He knew he was at a disadvantage since he wasn't strapped so he'd have to bow down to the youngin's gangsta if he wanted to see another day.

"Good!" D'Anthony said and blasted him in the shoulder.

"Aaarrrr!" the man screamed in agony, grabbing his shoulder and falling toward the ground dramatically. Before his body could meet the concrete, D'Anthony was hopping back inside the jack mobile and Chyna was pulling off.

"Now, you know it's tradition for new niggaz not to get a taste of the action their first time around but considering how you handled yourself tonight, I'm going to make an exception." Chyna grinned and handed him four bankrolls from the duffle bag. D'Anthony smiled, thanked him, and dapped him up. He stuffed the money inside the small zippered pouch of his backpack, tucked his pencil behind his ear, and laid back in his seat. He laid his navy blue Yankees fitted cap over his face and folded his arms *across his chest.* Chyna turned the volume up on Benny The Butcher's latest song and zipped through traffic.

When Chyna finally pulled up to the back of D'Anthony's school, he turned the volume down on the music and shook the young nigga awake. Taking his cap off his head, D'Anthony threw his head back, yawning and stretching. He put his baseball cap on backward and shook up with Chyna.

"A'ight, big homie, I'm up outta here but I'll catch you later on at the spot if Dolph gives the okay," D'Anthony said of Dolph accepting him into the Kings of Thieves.

"You ain't got nothing to worry about, my G. You're a shoo-in," Chyna told him. "You did yo' thang today. Plus, a nigga gon' vouch for you, nah mean?"

"No doubt," D'Anthony nodded, shaking up with him again. He slammed the door behind him and made his way over to the back gate. Chyna decided to wait until he hopped the gate and went inside before he left. As he watched him he couldn't help noticing the dingy yellow T-shirt that used to be white once upon a time he was wearing or the raggedy black Nike Cortez he was wearing. If it wasn't for him tangling rubber bands around them bitchez they'd be talking whenever he walked.

Chyna and D'Anthony came from the same circumstances. Two youths who were forced to do whatever they had to to survive in the slums. They lived right across the hall from each other in the Red Hook projects. Chyna had watched him and his three siblings grow up. They lived with their grandma who only got a social security check for herself and a welfare check for them. The money wasn't nearly enough to take care of three kids plus herself so D'Anthony hit the streets. He did everything from burglarizing homes to selling chopped-up Aspirin, passing it off as crack. Whatever dough he brought in to feed his family he gave it to his mother, telling her he'd earned the money shoveling snow or helping the elderly with their groceries. Although he wasn't lying, most of the bread he made came from the illegal hustles. He knew his grandma was a devoted Christian and if she knew that she wouldn't accept his dirty money. So he told her what he needed so she could sleep at night and still feel in favor of the Lord.

CHAPTER ELEVEN

Chyna knew about D'Anthony's family's financial hardships so he'd throw him a few dollars here and there whenever he came up on a lick. D'Anthony, who'd taken up the role of man of the house, felt less than taking money from someone he looked up to. So he started turning Chyna's charity down and asking him for work instead. The young nigga knew what crew Chyna ran under and he wanted to be a part of their organization. That way he could feed his family indefinitely.

Chyna whistled at D'Anthony and motioned him over. He jogged back to the car and ducked low to the passenger window.

"What's good, son?" D'Anthony asked curiously.

"I want chu to have somethin', and I'm not takin' no for an answer," Chyna told him, removing his Jordan 13s and sitting them on the passenger seat. He slipped his throwback Michael Jordan jersey over his head and passed it to him. He looked at the sneakers and the jersey and then at Chyna as he knew better than to give him anything he hadn't worked for.

"Yo', I appreciate the offer and all, but you already know my get down. I don't accept handouts. I—" The rest of D'Anthony's words died in his throat when Chyna sat his FN on his lap and shot daggers at him.

"My young nigga, it's either you accept these gifts I'm giving you, or this bullet as a consolation," Chyna told him straight up. "Which one will it be, young boy?" he asked, tapping his trigger finger against his black pistol.

D'Anthony stared at Chyna trying to see if he meant what he'd said. He had heard mad stories about him in the hood. Though there were lots about the good he had done. The overwhelming majority of them were about the wicked things he'd participated in. Nonetheless, D'Anthony didn't want to be on his bad side nor did he want a bullet in the face so he accepted his generosity.

"A'ight," D'Anthony replied, removing his backpack so he could put on the clothes.

"My nigga," Chyna smiled like Alonzo in Training Day. He watched D'Anthony get dressed in the items he'd given him. He then had him step back so he could see how he looked in them.

"That's crazy, yo."

"What's that?"

"You look better than me in my own shit."

D'Anthony smiled and shook his head. "Thanks, bro." he shook up with Chyna. Chyna tried to pull his hand back but he held fast. "Naw, Dunn, a young nigga really, really appreciate what you're doing for me. I don't know how I'll ever repay you."

"Between the two of us, I'm sure we'll think of something."

"Love, my G." A glassy-eyed D'Anthony told him, tapping his fist against his chest.

"Love," Chyna replied, returning the gesture. "I'll see you tonight, yo. Stay dangerous."

"All the time," D'Anthony said, walking away. Chyna blew his horn before pulling off, and he threw his hand over his head in response.

D'Anthony blinked back tears. Chyna had been showing him brotherly love and the feeling was euphoric. At that moment, whether or not Chyna knew it or not, he'd pledged his undying loyalty to him.

D'Anthony scaled the gate of his high school and jumped down to his bending knees. Holding the straps of his backpack, he trekked towards the building his class was being held in, glancing at the black digital timepiece that adorned his wrist. He realized his third-period class was about to be let out soon. He shrugged. His attitude was like fuck it! The way he saw it, school wasn't *paying the bills or putting food on the table so it could take a backseat to his hustle and grind.*

On my momma, I'll kill something behind Chyna. That's bro, bro, right there, D'Anthony thought. *He didn't know it then but he'd eventually have to prove that.* At that moment, the school's bell rang loud and annoyingly and teenagers poured out of the entrances of various tenements.

The King of Thieves Headquarters

Chyna, with his arm around D'Anthony's shoulders, led him into the master bedroom. The young nigga looked around curiously wondering why he'd been brought there. Chyna saw the look on his face from the corner of his eye as he took a drink from his Heineken.

"I know what chu thinkin' son, you don't even have to say it. You're thinkin' what the fuck are we doin' here, right?" Chyna smiled, holding the bottle loosely at his side.

D'Anthony nodded with a smile. "Yeah. What're you? A psychic or somethin'?"

"Nah, young nigga, I'ma king," Chyna flexed, showing the K.O.T. tattoo on his arm. "And you are, too." he nodded to the same ink on D'Anthony's arm. He glanced at it with a grin. Jayvon pulled out a small black box labeled MAGNUM and passed it to D'Anthony. "Tonight is the night a queen will welcome you home properly."

With that said, Chyna walked over to the bathroom adjacent to the master bedroom and opened the door. Standing aside, he took another drink of his Heneiken and one hell of a vision of a woman emerged. She was cute, light-skinned with freckles, and had the body of a Greek goddess. Devon, the young lady who had just come out of the bathroom, walked towards D'Anthony on her bare, pretty feet, staring at him hungrily between the braids hanging over her face. Her round, succulent breasts bounced as she advanced in his direction, rocking her hips from left to right. She had an expression on her face like she was about to eat D'Anthony alive.

***

The cab driver's horn blared, yanking D'Anthony out of his spiraling thoughts about Chyna. His eyes snapped to the windshield, just in time to see two kids dashing across the chaotic Los Angeles streets, narrowly avoiding a crushing fate under the relentless stream of traffic.

"Damn kids today, man, I swear," the driver grumbled, irritation dripping from every word as he shook his head. He kept on ranting, but D'Anthony's mind had already begun to drift, sleep creeping in like a thief. The driver adjusted the rearview mirror, maybe asking a question, but D'Anthony was too far gone, the heavy weight of exhaustion pulling him under.

***

L.A. traffic was hell, a suffocating beast that snarled and crawled at a snail's pace. The cab driver cursed under his breath, blaming the gridlock on the holiday rush—everyone trying to escape the city, to find a semblance of peace with their families. After nearly an hour of inching through the congestion, the airport finally came into view.

The driver took a long gulp from his Monster energy drink, trying to shake off the bone-deep fatigue of his sixteen-hour shift. "Man, these hours are kicking my brown ass," he muttered, his eyes flicking to the picture of his family wedged between the speedometer and dashboard. "But it's all gonna be worth it when I finally get enough to bring my wife and kids over."

He suddenly realized he didn't know which terminal D'Anthony needed. Glancing into the rearview mirror to ask, he saw the backseat still and silent. D'Anthony was slumped against the window, unmoving. A cold sweat broke out on the driver's forehead as he tried to rouse him, but D'Anthony didn't stir. Alarmed, he pulled over at the nearest terminal.

Just then, a black van with tinted windows and a sliding side door glided up behind the cab, its approach ghostly silent. Inside, two Kings, faces obscured by purple ski masks, gripped assault rifles with suppressors, eyes locked on their target. The plan was simple—quick, clean, and fatal. But as the cab driver yanked open the back door, D'Anthony's body tumbled out, lifeless and limp. His skin was ashen, eyes glazed over, as if death had claimed him in his sleep.

The driver's desperate cries for help pierced the air, his voice cracking as he shouted that D'Anthony was dead. The Kings in the van, poised to strike, froze. The job was done, but not by their hands. There was no honor in shooting a dead man. With a quick exchange of glances, they aborted the mission, the van slipping away as quietly as it had come.

CHAPTER TWELVE

Next day

Bag Man jumped up and stood upside-down, doing a split. He began his movements with a quick handstand to get in position. Then he started propelling himself from his feet, making his legs spin in rapid circles like the blades of a helicopter. Bag Man came back down on his feet and stood upright. Sweat rolled down his forehead as he breathed heavily. "You got that?"

Jayvon nodded. "I got it. The Spinning Helicopter Kick."

"Right. Now lemme see you try it."

"Okay," Jayvon said, visualizing himself performing the attack in his mind, hands ready. He took three quick breaths and then went for it. "Ooof," he groaned, hitting the side of his head and landing on his back.

Augustus, Chyna, and Chrissy stood in the background trying to contain their laughter.

"Boy, you've gotta be the sorriest son of a bitch I've ever had the misfortune of laying my stunningly brown bedroom eyes on. Get cho ass up," Bag Man pulled Jayvon up with both hands. "I don't care if we've gotta do this shit a million times, bitch. We're gonna nail it, and you're gonna come home with that bag, ya heard?"

Jayvon nodded.

"A'ight, youngin', pay close attention. I'ma lay down the demo again."

Once again, Bag Man performed the finishing move for Jayvon. When he felt like he didn't quite get it, he performed it once more. Jayvon nodded, letting him know he got the move.

"A'ight, you pathetic excuse for a man, have at it," Bag Man said, smacking dirt from his hands and rubbing them together.

"Okay, baby, you can do it. Whooo!" Chrissy screamed like a cheerleader, arms in the air, jumping up and down.

"Yeah. Big bro, you got this." Chyna egged him on, clapping.

"Thata boy, you got this!" Augustus yelled, holding his crutch up.

Jayvon attempted the Spinning Helicopter Kick again but collided with the ground before he could complete it. Determined, he hopped back up, bouncing around like a professional boxer, ready to throw down.

Jayvon attempted the Spinning Helicopter Kick for like the nine hundred and ninety-ninth time before finally completing it. He rose, shoulders slumped, breathing hard. He looked at Augustus, Chyna, and Chrissy. Chrissy and Augustus were snoring, their heads leaning on either of Chyna's shoulders while he was dozing off.

"Way to go, bitch! You did it, you finally fucking did it." Bag Man clapped excitedly and lifted Jayvon. He laughed heartily with his arms held high.

"He did it?" Chrissy asked, halfway asleep, wiping her eyes. Then it hit her that Jayvon had finally accomplished the finishing move he'd been working on for hours. "Holy shit. He finally fucking did it!" She shook Chyna and Augustus awake, informing them of Jayvon's accomplishment.

The fellas woke up one after the other. They were just as excited as she was. They hopped up and ran over to Jayvon, hugging and tossing him above their shoulders, then marched him back toward the house, their cheers echoing through the night.

As they carried Jayvon, laughter, and jubilation filled the air. The struggles and frustrations of the day melted away, replaced by a sense of triumph. They knew the road ahead was still fraught with challenges, but this victory, however small, was a testament to their perseverance.

***

Inside the house, they set Jayvon down, still basking in the glow of their shared achievement.

"I did that shit, unc," Jayvon said, a tired but triumphant smile on his face.

"Damn right, you did," Bag Man replied, clapping him on the back. "And tomorrow, we keep grinding. We've got a tournament to win."

Chrissy's eyes glinted with pride as she kissed Jayvon's cheek. "I knew you could do it." she addressed the rest of the gang. "I'm gonna go get dinner started."

"What's on the menu?" Bag Man asked.

"Catfish, spaghetti, and cornbread," Chrissy replied before disappearing inside the kitchen.

"Sounds damn good to me," Augustus said, taking the time to light up one of his funky ass cigars.

"Here he go with this shit," Bag Man scrunched his nose. Augustus put away his lighter and gave him the middle finger. "Fuck you back," he returned the gesture.

"Pause. Goddamn, unc." Chyna chimed in.

Jayvon laughed.

***

After dinner, Chrissy and Chyna headed inside the kitchen to wash the dishes, leaving Jayvon and Bag Man inside the dining room. Bag Man returned from taking a phone call. He sat down at the dining table wearing an expression as serious as a clogged artery.

"What's got your dick caught inna zipper?" Jayvon frowned when he saw the look on Bag Man's face.

"Bitch," Bag Man began, his voice low and intense, "I got word that a very dangerous man will be fighting in the tournament. He goes by the name Wild Child."

Jayvon brushed off Bag Man's warning. "Man, I've heard stories about this nigga before. I'm not worried."

Bag Man's fist slammed onto the dining room table, making the glasses clink and rattle. He scooted closer so only Jayvon could hear him, not wanting to worry Chyna and Chrissy. His eyes bore into Jayvon's with an intensity that couldn't be ignored.

"Listen to me," Bag Man hissed. "You'll be going toe to toe with the Grim Reaper in the flesh. Wild Child is a monster, and if you're gonna beat a monster, you have to become one."

Jayvon's confidence wavered as he took in Bag Man's words. He had never seen him this serious.

"For every punch he throws, you gotta throw two," Bag Man continued. "For however hard he tries to hit you, you have to hit his bitch-ass twice as hard. No, fuck that, three times as hard. You've gotta break something inside that son of a bitch." To emphasize his point, Bag Man angrily smacked a nearby glass of water, launching it against the wall.

The sound of the impact echoed in the silent room, and Jayvon realized the gravity of the situation.

"You fellas alright in there?" Chrissy called out from the kitchen.

"Yep. Yo' bonehead fiancé just accidentally knocked over a glass," Augustus interjected. He was like a ghost. No one knew he was in the dining room besides Bag Man.

Jayvon glanced over his shoulder at Augustus, who stood with his arms folded across his chest, leaning on his crutch. He wore an expression just as serious as Bag Man's.

Jayvon tried to hide his apprehension, but he couldn't shake the feeling of dread creeping into his gut. "I'm gonna get back to training," he mumbled, excusing himself from the table.

"I'm going with chu," Bag Man said, rising to his feet.

Augustus followed closely behind them, his crutches thudding softly against the floor. They left Chyna and Chrissy in the kitchen, washing dishes and reminiscing about old times.

***

Backyard

Jayvon's earlier confidence was now laced with an urgent need to prepare. He threw himself into his training with renewed vigor, every punch and kick driven by the fear and anticipation of facing Wild Child.

Bag Man watched closely, his eyes never leaving Jayvon. "Bitch, you needa focus. Wild Child isn't just another opponent, this muthafucka issa savage."

Augustus, leaning on his crutches, added, "I made a couple of calls, my guys say this bastard's fists are legendary. You gotta be ready for 'em, kid."

Jayvon nodded as sweat dripped from his brow. "I got this. I'll be ready."

***

Meanwhile

Chyna and Chrissy continued washing dishes, their conversation light and nostalgic. They were blissfully unaware of the heavy conversation that had just taken place.

"Yo, I swear to god, I ain't never seen a nigga run that fast in my life," Chyna laughed, scrubbing a plate.

Chrissy chuckled. "Stop. You've got me laughing so hard in here I'm passing gas."

"Wait. That came outta yo' ass? Thank god. 'Cause I thought that came outta yo' mouth. Shiit." Chyna smiled like the Joker.

"Shut up," Chrissy playfully punched Chyna's arm.

***

As the night wore on, Jayvon's movements grew sharper, more precise. Each punch, each kick, was a testament to his dedication and the weight of Bag Man's words. He knew going against Wild Child would be the ultimate test, but he also knew he couldn't back down.

Bag Man stepped closer, placing a hand on Jayvon's shoulder. "We're with chu. Every step of the way."

Jayvon nodded with a hardening expression. "Thanks. I won't let chu old niggaz down."

Augustus, watching from the sidelines, gave a supportive nod. "We've got your back. Just give it everything you've got."

***

The trio trained late into the night, pushing Jayvon to his limits and beyond. The stakes were higher than ever, but they were determined to be ready. As they finally wrapped up, the exhaustion was evident on Jayvon's face, but so was the fire in his eyes.

"Your ready," Bag Man said, clapping Jayvon on the back.

Jayvon looked at his friends, feeling a surge of gratitude. "I am ready, ready to kick some ass."

***

Chyna and Chrissy finished up, oblivious to the intense preparations happening in the backyard. They dried the last of the dishes, their laughter fading into the night.

Jayvon, Bag Man, and Augustus enter the mansion,, the weight of the upcoming tournament on their shoulders. They knew that the days ahead would be filled with challenges, but they were ready to face them.

CHAPTER THIRTEEN

Finesse's luggage was packed for Bali, a trip he eagerly anticipated. Instead of a suit, he opted for something casual yet stylish: a black bubble vest, a Nike cap, and a pair of rugged ACG boots. He accessorized with a pair of princess-cut diamond earrings and twin tennis necklaces, one longer than the other, both gleaming against his chest. Satisfied with his reflection in the mirror, he called his chauffeur to pull the stretch Mercedes around to the front of his mansion. With a confident stride, he made his way down the grand staircase.

At the base of the stairs, Roderick, his ever-dutiful butler, stood ready with a silver platter bearing a glass of Finesse's favorite bourbon and his favorite brand of cigar. Finesse took a slow sip, savoring the rich, smoky flavor, and then allowed Roderick to place the cigar between his lips and light it with a flourish. He drew in a deep breath and let the smoke fill his lungs before exhaling a perfect cloud.

When he stepped outside, the sleek black Mercedes was waiting on him, its exterior gleaming under the mansion's portico. His chauffeur, an elderly white gentleman with a distinguished air, held the back door open and gave him a respectful nod. Returning the gesture, Finesse slid into the car, feeling the cool and inviting plush black leather interior.

A stunning woman was waiting for him inside. Her smooth chocolate skin glowed with an inner radiance, and her long, silky hair framed her exquisitely beautiful face. Her figure, reminiscent of Jessica Rabbit's iconic curves, was accentuated by a form-fitting black dress that showcased her ample cleavage. She wore dazzling earrings, a sparkling platinum necklace, and a luxurious mink coat that added an extra touch of glamour.

"Hey there, handsome," she purred, with a smooth, seductive melody of a voice.

"Well, aren't you a sight for sore eyes," Finesse replied with a widening grin, settling beside her.

An intoxicating scent expelled from her as she leaned in and whispered, "Ready for our adventure?"

"More than ready," Finesse replied, taking her hand and kissing it gently. "Let's make this trip unforgettable," he unzipped his jeans. She pulled out his meat and got down to business.

Swallowing the last of his alcohol, he closed his eyes as he laid his head back, licking his lips. "Oooh, oooh, oooh. Watch those teeth, baby, much better." he melted into the seat and enjoyed the blessing she placed upon him.

***

Finesse's date for the Bali trip was already asleep, her head resting gently against the plush seat as the private jet lifted into the friendly skies. The hum of the engines and the luxury of the cabin made for a serene atmosphere, but Finesse's mind was anything but calm. Tossing back a handful of peanuts, he stared out the window at the shrinking lights below, his thoughts swirling with anticipation and a hint of malice.

He was confident this trip would be one for the books, but what would make it truly unforgettable was the chance to cross paths with Chrissy, or at the very least, someone she loved. He imagined the satisfaction of forcing her whereabouts out of them and exacting a long-overdue revenge for her betrayal.

Nah, I've done too much in my life for God to bless me like that. I'm not even gon' get my hopes up, Finesse thought as he finished his bag of peanuts. The memory of Chrissy's treachery gnawed at him, but he pushed it aside, focusing instead on the journey ahead.

He signaled the flight attendant and requested a pillow. "Don't wake us until we've landed," he instructed, settling back into his seat. Closing his eyes, he let the gentle rocking of the plane lull him towards sleep, the soft murmur of the engines a soothing backdrop.

Little did he know, the Almighty had a surprise in store for him in Bali. A twist of fate was waiting to unfold, one that would bring him face to face with the past he so desperately wanted to confront.

***

Bali/ Fight night

The line outside the mansion stretched under the dim glow of streetlights. The crowd shifted restlessly as they waited to be granted access. The estate loomed in the background, its dark silhouette a fortress of secrets and power, casting long shadows that seemed to reach out like an octopus's tentacles.

Bartise's Bali mansion was an empire of indulgence, sprawling across acres like a kingdom unto itself. It was a spectacle: roller coasters weaving through lush gardens, bumper cars zipping across neon-lit arenas, and water slides spiraling into crystalline pools. This wasn't just a mansion—it was a playground for the wealthy and powerful, a place where opulence and thrill met in a seamless blend.

The mansion was fortified with security guards in tactical vests, armed with MP-5s, stationed at every corner. These weren't just showpieces; they were highly trained operatives, ready to neutralize any threat. The entrance was a marvel of modern technology—guests, dressed in their finest, paid their entry fees digitally before being subjected to rigorous searches. Every person and item was scrutinized, and scanned by cutting-edge metal detectors that left no room for error.

Among the first wave of guests was Finesse and his stunning companion. Finesse knew better than to underestimate Bartise's security. The Glock he'd purchased from a street hustler was quickly discarded when he saw the thoroughness of the checks. He needed to stay armed, but getting a gun past the detectors was out of the question.

With quick thinking and ruthless efficiency, Finesse melted down plastic utensils in a hotel room microwave, fashioning them into a crude but effective 8-inch knife. It wasn't elegant, but it was deadly—and more importantly, undetectable. He handed the knife to his date, who slipped it into her bag with the ease of someone used to hiding dangerous secrets. As they passed through security, Finesse felt a surge of satisfaction—they were in, and they were armed.

As they entered the main grounds, his date leaned in close and whispered, "You think this lil' plastic toy will save us if shit hits the fan?"

Finesse smirked as he scanned the crowd. "It's not about saving us, baby. It's about making sure they don't see us coming."

***

Luka, LaDecia, Delroy, and their crew approached the mansion next, their plan meticulously crafted. They knew Bartise's event would be a fortress, with security measures that could detect even the smallest threat. But Luka was no stranger to impossible missions.

The team was armed with non-metallic knives, ceramic blades, and other tools designed to evade detection. Their weapons were hidden in plain sight, tucked into the folds of clothing, and disguised as everyday items. As they passed through the checkpoint, Luka exchanged a glance with LaDecia. They were confident, ready for whatever lay ahead.

Once inside, Luka and LaDecia took in their surroundings. Delroy, always observant, began scrolling through the betting device they had been handed at the entrance. The screen displayed the fighters' profiles, with rotating images and detailed stats.

As Delroy swiped through the options, one image made him pause. He handed the device to Luka and LaDecia, pointing at the screen. "Look, it's him. Wild Child, uh, I mean Neo."

Luka and LaDecia leaned in, their eyes narrowing as they examined the image. At first, they weren't sure. The fighter was tall and muscular, his face hardened by years of combat. But then the image rotated, revealing the fighter's shoulder—and there it was, the unmistakable birthmark Luka had given his son the night he was born.

LaDecia's breath caught in her throat. "It's him," she whispered, relief and anguish flooding her voice.

Luka's jaws tightened, his eyes locking onto the image of the boy they had lost so long ago. "Our son," he murmured, his voice dripping with emotion.

Watching them closely, Delroy sensed the weight of the moment. "Now we know for sure," he said. "We've found 'em."

***

Unbeknownst to Luka, LaDecia, Delroy, and their entourage, Jayvon, and Bag Man was just a few invites behind, quietly blending in with the crowd. They weren't here to make a scene, not yet. There was a calculated patience in their posture, a readiness that spoke volumes about what was to come.

Chyna had already slipped away, moving with a purpose as he tossed Bag Man's bamboo staff—his deadly katana—over the mansion's fence. The move was quick, precise, and necessary. The staff, now hidden, would be waiting for them inside, a silent promise of the violence that would follow.

When Chyna returned, Bag Man's eyes locked onto him, a silent question hanging in the air.

"You stash it?" Bag Man asked.

"Yeah, over the fence. Easy to grab once we're in," Chyna responded. His voice was steady, but his gaze was sharp, scanning the area like a predator on the hunt.

Bag Man focused on Jayvon, noticing something visibly wrong with him. "You okay, youngsta?"

Jayvon forced a grin, trying to play it off. "Okay? Shiiit, I'm fuckin' fantastic."

Bag Man wasn't one to be fooled. He had known Jayvon for too long and had seen him in too many situations where the stakes were just as high, if not higher. The tension in Jayvon's stance, the slight clenching of his fists—these were all signs that Bag Man picked up on, no matter how hard Jayvon tried to mask them.

"Bitch, you've gotta be the worst fuckin' liar to ever fuckin' lie in a room full of the biggest fuckin' liars in the history of fuckin' lying," Bag Man said, his voice tinged with amusement and seriousness. "Now you know better than to lie to me and Baby Brother. We've known you long enough to see when something's bugging you."

Jayvon couldn't help chuckling, the tension easing just a bit. "Okay, okay. You got me. I'm a lil' nervous about this tournament, but I think it's normal."

Chyna's expression softened, but his words carried weight. "It most certainly is. But it's good to have a bit of fear, bro. Fear of the unknown? That shit keeps you on point. It keeps you on yo' toes and ready for anythang that comes yo' way."

There was a pause, the words sinking in, not just as advice but as a truth Jayvon couldn't deny. He nodded with a newfound determination hardening his eyes. "You should've been a pimp, Unc. You got a way with words."

Chyna smirked with a flicker of dark humor in his gaze. "Maybe in another life, Scrap. But for now, I'm just here to make sure you're ready to kick some ass."

CHAPTER FOURTEEN

Jayvon felt a surge of confidence, the nerves that had been gnawing at his insides now transformed into a sharp focus. He wasn't just stepping into a tournament—he was walking into a war zone, and with Bag Man and Chyna by his side, he knew he was equipped for battle.

As they moved forward in line, the tension around them thickened, each step bringing them closer to the unknown dangers waiting inside the mansion. The estate was more than just a venue; it was a battleground, and the people inside were either predators or prey.

The night was alive with the sounds of the city—distant sirens, the hum of traffic, the low murmur of conversations blending into a cacophony that seemed to mirror the chaos brewing beneath the surface. But amidst all of it, Jayvon felt a strange calm settle over him, the kind that only comes when you're ready to face whatever the hell was about to break loose.

And when the gates finally opened, it wasn't just a step forward—it was the crossing of a threshold into something darker, something far more dangerous than anyone outside those gates could understand.

Each guest was handed a sleek device, 7-inches long and 5-inches wide. These gadgets weren't just for placing bets on the upcoming fights—they were detailed dossiers on the fighters, complete with visuals, stats, and skill sets. The guests studied their options, analyzing odds, and strategizing their bets. The thrill of potential fortune and the ever-present undercurrent of danger created an electrifying atmosphere.

***

The guests mingled, placing their bets and sharing knowing glances, but beneath the surface, everyone knew this wasn't just a game. This was a high-stakes battle where the price of failure could be fatal.

Finesse and his date navigated the crowd with ease, their eyes always moving, always alert. Luka, LaDecia, and their crew blended in seamlessly, their faces a perfect mask of calm as they sized up the competition and surveyed the gathering. Every detail mattered—every exit, every security guard, every potential threat.

The lights dimmed, casting long shadows across the mansion's ornate decor. The air thickened with anticipation as the first fight was announced. The crowd's chatter quieted, replaced by the hum of excitement and the tension of what was to come. The fighters' names flashed across the guests' betting devices, and eyes quickly scanned the screens, calculating odds, and assessing risks.

Luka, holding the device that had revealed the truth about Wild Child, exchanged a glance with LaDecia. A silent agreement passed between them.

The atmosphere shifted, becoming almost electric, as the fighters stepped into the ring. This was more than just a fight—it was a show of power, a spectacle of violence that would set the tone for the rest of the night.

As the first punch was thrown, the night's true nature began to reveal itself. In Bartise's mansion, alliances would be tested, betrayals executed, and only the cunning would emerge victorious. The games had begun, and there was no turning back.

Bartise sat on his ornate throne, symbolizing his dominance and wealth, with Purp on one side and Stutter-Box on the other. The golden cup in his hand, encrusted with colorful stones, gleamed in the low light as he took a sip, savoring the moment. The arena was alive with anticipation, every eye on the powerful drug lord as he prepared to announce the next fighters.

"The next bout," Bartise declared, his voice commanding attention, "is one you've all been waiting for."

Instantly, the crowd erupted into a frenzy. Cheers, hollers, and whistles filled the air. The energy was electric, the excitement palpable as the audience leaned forward in anticipation.

***

LaDecia's heart pounded in her chest as she locked eyes with the figure emerging from the shadows. It was Wild Child, striding into the arena to the thumping bass of Brand Nubian's "Punks Jump Up to Get Beat Down." His presence was commanding, even more so in his hooded polyester robe, adorned with illustrations of bleeding claw marks. The bold letters of his name were clenched inside the snarling mouth of a panther on his back, a symbol of his ferocity.

Recognition flickered like a flame in LaDecia's mind, the memories rushing back—memories of the night she gave birth to him, of the pain and joy intertwined. Her instincts screamed at her to run to him, to throw her arms around him, to tell him how much she loved and missed him every single day.

But she didn't move. She couldn't. Her heart ached, but her resolve held firm. Bartise owned Wild Child, and she knew he wouldn't let go of his prized fighter easily. If she and her family wanted him back, they would have to fight for him, to go to war with the drug lord and his empire. The path to peace was soaked in blood, and she knew it.

McGuiness, Wild Child's trainer, appeared behind him, helping him remove the robe and draping it over his arm. The trainer stepped back, his eyes focused on his fighter, watching as Wild Child stretched and bounced on the balls of his feet, readying himself for the brutal contest ahead.

***

The crowd's roar reached new heights as Juggernaut Jones was announced. The six-foot-three terror emerged, flanked by two stunning white women dressed identically to him. His crimson cape with gold-spiked shoulder pads glittered under the lights, a menacing display that matched his deadly reputation. His hairstyle, reminiscent of Blade the Vampire Slayer, only added to his imposing aura.

The crowd's cheers intensified as the two women moved to either side of him, assisting in the dramatic removal of his cape. Through the reflective lenses of his shades, Juggernaut Jones surveyed the crowd, his gaze as cold and calculating as ever. With a smirk, he removed the shades and hurled them into the audience, a cocky gesture that sent the crowd into another wave of applause and whistles.

As the white women proceeded to rub his muscular body down with baby oil, Juggernaut made his pecs jump up and down, each ripple of muscle met with wild cheers from the audience. He was putting on a show, feeding off the crowds' energy and basking in their adoration. But beneath the theatrics was a deadly fighter, one who relished in the violence and the spectacle.

***

LaDecia watched with her fists clenched at her sides. Wild Child, her son, was about to face a man built like a tank. This was a man who enjoyed the brutal dance of combat as much as the adulation of the crowd. She knew this was no ordinary fight—it was a battle that would determine more than just victory in the arena. It would decide the fate of her family, of the son she had lost and now found.

But for now, she held her composure. There would be time for tears and reunions later.

Juggernaut Jones and Wild Child squared off. The crowd was on its feet and roaring in excitement at the violence to come.

Jayvon, Chyna, and Bag Man stood on the sidelines, the electric buzz of the crowd nearly overwhelming. The fight between Wild Child and Juggernaut Jones was a savage display of brutality. Wild Child moved like a shadow, slipping through Juggernaut's defenses with unnatural speed. Each punch he threw landed with bone-crushing force, leaving Juggernaut gasping and stumbling.

The final blow was a merciless punctuation mark to the fight. Wild Child's fist smashed into Juggernaut's cheek with a sickening crack. Juggernaut was sent hurtling through the air, his body twisting grotesquely before he crashed into the ground, blood spewing from his mouth and nose. The crowd's roar reached a fever pitch as two white women ran to Juggernaut's side, their faces painted with panic. They shook him violently, trying to rouse him, while EMTs rushed in with a gurney. They carefully loaded Juggernaut onto it, the women trailing behind them, their frantic cries cutting through the chaos as the EMTs wheeled him out.

With Juggernaut gone, Bartise's voice boomed over the arena. "Next fight: Bloody Knuckles versus King Smite!"

The crowd erupted in anticipation as King Smite made his entrance. He was a striking figure: a Caucasian with long, flowing blonde hair and piercing blue eyes that seemed to cut through the dim light. His full beard and muscular frame gave him a nearly mythic presence. He wore a gold, jewel-studded crown and a lion's hide draped over his shoulders, the beast's head still attached, eyes glaring lifelessly.

King Smite drank from a golden goblet, then spat the liquor into the crowd with a roguish grin. He tossed the goblet aside with a flourish and struck a dramatic pose, his long tongue extended and his eyes wide. The crowd went wild, feeding off his larger-than-life persona.

Jayvon's gaze locked onto Wild Child, who stood on the sidelines, arms folded across his chest. Wild Child's eyes were cold, his stare unblinking as the two men locked eyes. The tension between them was palpable. Wild Child tilted his head toward King Smite, a clear gesture for Jayvon to focus on the fight ahead. Jayvon met his gaze with a fierce intensity and mouthed, "Yo ass is next, nigga." Wild Child's lips curved into a satisfied smirk, and he gave a dismissive nod as if to say, "Yeah, whatever, mothafucka."

King Smite slowly removed his crown and placed it on the head of an old, wrinkled Black lady standing on the sidelines. He draped the lion's hide over her frail shoulders, the weight of it almost too much for her to bear. He tapped his cheek for a kiss, which she planted with trembling lips. King Smite then turned to Jayvon, drawing a thumb across his throat in a deadly gesture, his blue eyes locked on his opponent's.

Jayvon rolled his shoulders, cracking his neck as he beckoned King Smite to the center of the battleground. The crowd's noise swelled as the two fighters faced off, the tension so thick it was almost suffocating.

The bell rang, and the two men clashed like titans. King Smite came out swinging, his fists like sledgehammers. Jayvon dodged the first few strikes, feeling the wind of each near miss. King Smite's punches were relentless, a flurry of power and aggression that pushed Jayvon back. But Jayvon wasn't about to be outdone. He ducked under a wide hook and drove his fist into King Smite's ribs with a satisfying crack. King Smite grunted but didn't back down, he responded with a knee to Jayvon's gut, knocking the wind out of him.

CHAPTER FIFTEEN

Jayvon stumbled back, gasping for air, but King Smite was on him in a flash, his fists raining down like a hailstorm. Jayvon blocked as best he could, his arms absorbing the brunt of the attack, but the force was brutal. His muscles screamed in pain, but he refused to fall.

In a sudden burst of energy, Jayvon caught King Smite off guard. He sidestepped a vicious punch and landed a hard uppercut to King Smite's jaw, snapping his head back. Seizing the moment, Jayvon unleashed a flurry of punches to King Smite's torso, each blow driving him back step by step. The crowd was on their feet, roaring with excitement as Jayvon pressed the attack.

King Smite, snarling in fury, swung wildly, but Jayvon ducked under it, pivoting behind him. With a savage growl, Jayvon grabbed King Smite from behind, lifting him off his feet. The crowd gasped as Jayvon hoisted King Smite high above his head, muscles straining with the effort. He turned to face Wild Child, who watched with a bored expression, arms still folded.

Jayvon held King Smite up for a moment longer, letting the weight of the moment sink in. Wild Child yawned, a mocking gesture that sent a surge of rage through Jayvon. With a roar, Jayvon slammed King Smite down on the ground, the impact shaking the surface. But he wasn't done. Jayvon leaped into the air, coming down hard with a Leg Drop, the back of his knee crashing onto King Smite's chest with a bone-crunching thud.

King Smite's body convulsed, the air knocked out of him as he lay on the asphalt, gasping for breath. Jayvon stood over him, victorious, his chest heaving as he stared down at Wild Child. The crowd's roar was deafening, but Jayvon didn't hear anything. He was locked in on Wild Child, who smirked and waved him off as if dismissing him as just another contender.

Jayvon's heart pounded in his chest as he stepped back from King Smite, his victory tainted by the knowledge that the real fight was still to come. He had made his statement, but Wild Child's reaction was a brutal reminder that this was just the beginning.

***

The night raged on with a fury that only grew stronger as fight after fight passed. The arena was a cauldron of sweat, blood, and screams, and Jayvon and Wild Child watched every match with cold, calculating eyes. Each victory brought them closer to the inevitable showdown that everyone in the crowd was waiting for. They tore through their opponents like predators, leaving nothing but broken bodies in their wake.

Finally, the moment came. Only two men were left standing. Jayvon and Wild Child faced each other in the center of the ring, the crowd's anticipation so thick it was almost suffocating. This was more than just a fight—it was a war, and the prize wasn't just the millions on the line. It was about respect, about proving who truly ruled this savage world.

The bell rang, and they clashed with a ferocity that shook the very foundations of the arena. The opening exchanges were fast and brutal, each man throwing punches and kicks with deadly intent. Jayvon was quick, his fists like lightning, and he managed to slip past Wild Child's defenses more than once, landing solid hits to the body and face. But Wild Child was unfazed, absorbing the punishment like a machine and returning fire with twice the force.

They circled each other, breathing heavily, each man searching for an opening. Jayvon feinted to the left and then came in hard with a right hook, but Wild Child saw it coming. He ducked under the punch and drove his knee into Jayvon's gut with bone-crunching force. Jayvon gasped, doubling over, but before he could recover, Wild Child's elbow crashed down on the back of his neck, sending him sprawling to the mat.

Jayvon scrambled back to his feet, blood dripping from his nose. He shook his head to clear the cobwebs and then came at Wild Child again, this time with a vicious uppercut that connected with Wild Child's jaw, snapping his head back. The crowd erupted as Wild Child stumbled, but he recovered quickly, his eyes blazing with fury. He charged at Jayvon, tackling him to the ground in a savage display of power.

The two men grappled on the ground, each trying to gain the upper hand. Finally, Wild Child managed to pin Jayvon down, and rain punches on his face. Jayvon's world exploded in pain as Wild Child's fists connected, splitting skin and rattling bone. But Jayvon wasn't done yet. With a surge of adrenaline, he managed to twist his body and throw Wild Child off him, rolling back to his feet.

They squared off again, both men battered and bloodied but far from beaten. Jayvon knew he couldn't let Wild Child get the upper hand again. He launched a relentless barrage of punches and kicks, pushing Wild Child back toward the ropes. But Wild Child was a wall, blocking or deflecting most of the blows, waiting for the right moment to strike back.

And then he found it. Jayvon overcommitted to a right cross, and Wild Child sidestepped it, delivering a devastating counterpunch to Jayvon's ribs. The impact was like being hit by a sledgehammer, and Jayvon felt something crack. He gasped, staggering back, his vision blurring from the pain. Wild Child didn't give him a chance to recover. He pressed his advantage, hitting Jayvon with a brutal combination of punches to the body and head, each one landing with precision and power.

Jayvon's legs wobbled as he tried to stay on his feet, but Wild Child was relentless. A powerful left hook smashed into Jayvon's jaw, spinning him around. His head snapped back, and he stumbled, barely able to stay upright. Wild Child moved in for the kill, his eyes cold and merciless. He grabbed Jayvon by the shoulders and drove his knee into Jayvon's midsection again and again, each blow sending shockwaves of pain through his body.

Jayvon tried to fight back, but his strength was fading. Wild Child's assault was too much. A crushing right cross to the temple finally brought Jayvon to his knees. He swayed with his vision swimming, the world around him becoming a blur of lights and noise. He could barely see Wild Child anymore, just a shadowy figure looming over him. His mind flashed back to the doctor's words: *Death or permanently blind.*

Desperation clawed at Jayvon as he tried to rise, but his body wouldn't obey. Wild Child took a step back, measuring his next move, then unleashed a final, devastating kick to Jayvon's head. The impact was like an explosion, and Jayvon's world went dark. He collapsed to the mat, his breath ragged, his vision completely gone. He couldn't tell if his eyes were open or closed. The only thing he could hear was the distant roar of the crowd, now just a dull, fading noise in the back of his mind.

***

In the depths of unconsciousness, Jayvon found himself in a dimly lit movie theater. The air smelled of buttery popcorn, and beside him were Chrissy, Chyna, Bag Man, and Augustus, all laughing like they didn't have a care in the world. They were shoving fistfuls of popcorn into their mouths, washing it down with cherry slushies, their eyes glued to the screen where the latest comedy flick played. Jayvon couldn't help but join in, his deep laughter mixing with theirs, almost forgetting the world outside.

But then, without warning, the screen flickered, the happy scenes of the movie glitching and warping into something darker. Jayvon's laughter died in his throat as the image on the screen shifted to a shot of him lying on the cold, hard ground—Wild Child standing over him, triumphant.

"What the fuck?" Jayvon mumbled, eyes wide, popcorn spilling from his lips as he stared at the screen in disbelief. He turned to his friends, but they were gone, vanished into the shadows as if they had never been there. The theater was empty now, the only sound was the thudding of his heartbeat, growing louder, pounding in his ears.

His eyes snapped back to the screen. There, he saw Chyna and Bag Man screaming for him to get up, their faces twisted with desperation. Meanwhile, Wild Child strutted around, arms raised high, basking in the cheers of the bloodthirsty crowd. The scene on the screen burned itself into Jayvon's mind—a vision of defeat, of everything he feared. The screen abruptly went black, but his heartbeat remained, echoing in the darkness.

Jayvon stood, his body tense, eyes locked on the empty screen. Then, out of the blackness, his family appeared, their faces illuminated by a faint, ghostly light. They were calling out to him, urging him to rise, to fight, reminding him of everything he had to live for. The screen played scenes from their lives together—moments of joy, pain, struggle, and triumph. One by one, they began to fade away, until only Bag Man was left. He had a serious face and his eyes were blazing with intensity.

Suddenly, Bag Man's face filled the entire screen. He appeared larger than life and his voice boomed through the theater. "Get back up on yo' feet, you stankin' bitch, you! This fight ain't over yet!" he shouted like a commanding officer, spit flying from his lips. His voice echoed throughout the movie theater.

**

Jayvon's eyes snapped open like a man resurrected. His vision was cloudy, the world around him hazy and distorted, but it didn't matter. He could see enough to finish this fight. Slowly and painfully, he pushed himself up from the ground and his muscles screamed in protest. Bag Man and Chyna erupted in wild cheers, hugging each other like they'd just witnessed a miracle.

"That's what I'm talkin' about, lil' baby! My boy is back!" Bag Man hollered, throwing phantom punches alongside Chyna, both dancing excitedly. "Whoop his ass, kid! Show 'em what I taught cha!"

The crowd's roar swelled to a deafening pitch as Jayvon got back to his feet. He squinted through the haze, trying to focus on Wild Child, who was already swaggering his way. Jayvon raised his fists, a slow, confident smile spreading across his battered face.

CHAPTER SIXTEEN

"Don't go countin' that bag up yet, Wild Child," Jayvon said, his voice steady and full of menace. "Daddy's 'bouta spank that ass."

Wild Child sneered, his fists coming up as he slid into his fighting stance. "You gon' have to show me, better than you can tell me," he spat back, eyes locked on Jayvon with murderous intent.

Wild Child lunged forward, a blur of motion as he unleashed a barrage of punches, his fists flying like a swarm of angry hornets. Jayvon's instincts took over, his body moving on autopilot as he dodged and weaved, slipping past each punch with precision. Wild Child was fast, but Jayvon was faster. He countered with a series of bone-crunching punches of his own, each one landing with devastating force. The final blow in his flurry caught Wild Child square on the jaw, sending him stumbling back, blood dripping from his lips.

Wild Child snarled like a wounded animal, wiping the blood away, his eyes wild with rage. He charged at Jayvon again, veins bulging from his forehead as he let out a primal scream. Jayvon stood his ground, his mind sharp despite the fog in his vision. He closed his eyes, focusing on the sound of Wild Child's bare feet slapping against the asphalt as he closed in.

At the last possible second, Jayvon spun on his heel, delivering a perfectly timed Spinning Helicopter Kick—the move Bag Man had drilled into him over and over. His heel connected with Wild Child's jaw, sending blood and sweat flying everywhere. Wild Child flew aside like a tackling dummy, crashing to the ground hard.

The arena fell silent, the crowd stunned as they watched Wild Child lay defeated. Jayvon stood tall, chest heaving, eyes locked on his fallen opponent. He had done it. Against all odds, he had risen from the brink of defeat and knocked Wild Child down for good.

Chyna and Bag Man's faces lit up and they ran out onto the battleground. They lifted Jayvon onto their shoulders, parading him around as the crowd began to cheer. Jayvon, his vision clearing slightly, looked down at his friends, a weary but triumphant smile spreading across his face.

"You did it, Scrap!" Chyna shouted, his voice barely audible over the roar of the crowd.

"That's what I'm talking about!" Bag Man yelled, beaming with pride.

Amid the celebration, Wild Child, barely conscious of the brutal blow to his jaw, struggled to get up. An annoying siren rang loudly in his ears, throwing him off balance. He looked like he was trying to stay on his feet during an earthquake. Just as he was about to fall again, a pair of strong arms caught him.

Wild Child looked up and saw a man who mirrored him in appearance, except he was older and more formidable. The man was a shade darker with a crown of salt-and-pepper curls and a thick beard, trimmed to godlike perfection.

"You okay, son?" the man asked concerned.

"Son?" Wild Child asked, frowning in confusion.

The man nodded and turned to a beautiful woman standing beside him. "And this is your mother," he said, sweeping his hand toward his lovely wife.

Wild Child looked at her and instantly recognized where he got his striking eyes and 3c textured hair. She had the same eyes, filled with tears, and hair that cascaded down her shoulders.

"Yes, Neo, it is I, baby boy," LaDecia said, her voice trembling as she held his face gently in her hands. Tears burst from Wild Child's eyes as he sniffled. He'd finally met his parents. His dream had come true.

"But how do you know you're my biological parents?" Wild Child asked, looking from his father to his mother, still in shock.

LaDecia smiled through her tears. "You have a birthmark scar on your shoulder," she explained. "It's shaped like an L with another L upside down. Those are the initials of Luka and LaDecia. We marked all of our children this way so we could find them after they'd been sold. We even named you Neo."

Luka nodded, placing a comforting hand on his son's shoulder. "We never stopped looking for you. And now we've found you."

Wild Child—or Neo—looked at the scar on his shoulder, the same birthmark he had always wondered about. The realization that these people were indeed his parents hit him hard, and he hugged them both tightly.

"And these are your siblings," LaDecia said, gesturing behind her.

Neo turned to see six young men and women, all dressed in designer brands like their parents. Each one of them stepped forward and revealed the same birthmark Luka gave them at birth. They then introduced themselves and hugged Neo tightly.

"We've been waiting for this moment," said one of his brothers, a tall man with a kind smile.

"Welcome home, bro," said a sister with sparkling eyes.

Neo felt overwhelmed with emotion. He had never imagined he would find his family in such a dramatic and unexpected way. The years of feeling alone and lost were suddenly washed away by the warmth and love of his newfound family.

As the crowd slowly began to disperse, Jayvon, still bruised and battered from the fight, watched the reunion from a distance. Chyna, Bag Man, and Chrissy stood beside him, sharing in the joy of the moment.

"Looks like homie's found some long-lost relatives," Jayvon said with a satisfied smile.

Chyna nodded. "Least he got something more than an ass-whupping outta this."

Jayvon grinned at Chyna and shook his head.

Bag Man clapped Jayvon on the back. "You did good out there, bitch. You've gotta lotta heart."

Jayvon winced slightly but smiled. "Thanks, B. I couldn't have done it without chu though," he dapped him up.

Bag Man smiled. "Yeah. I know. I'm fuckin' amazing." He held his head high and strutted around arrogantly.

As the crowd's cheers began to die down, Wild Child, battered and bruised, walked over to where Jayvon and them stood. Jayvon, still on edge, braced himself for another confrontation. His body was tense yet ready. But to his surprise, instead of Wild Child throwing a punch, he extended his hand.

Jayvon's eyes searched Wild Child's face for any sign of hostility. He didn't find any so he reached out and shook his hand firmly.

"Congrats on your victory," Wild Child said with a strained but genuine voice. "You got me good with that kick. Once I heal up, I'm coming for that rematch, big dawg."

Jayvon grinned and the tension eased from his body. "I'll be ready. We'll make it one to remember."

Wild Child nodded, then turned to introduce his newfound family. "Everyone, this is my family. My father, Luka, and my mother, LaDecia. And these are my siblings," he said proudly, gesturing to the group around him.

Jayvon, Chyna, and Bag Man exchanged introductions and friendly greetings with Wild Child and his family. The atmosphere shifted from one of competition to camaraderie.

In a domino effect, the devices that were given out before the tournament began to chime, and everyone who bet on Jayvon to win looked at them happily.

"Looks like that check just cleared, big bro," Chyna said, showing Jayvon and Bag Man the $5,000,000 that just hit their account.

The reality of Wild Child's defeat sank into Bartise's brain. The arena was caught in stunned silence. The cheers that had erupted moments before faded into a tense and heavy quiet. All eyes turned to Bartise who had anger and disbelief etched into his features. He had bet on Wild Child, the undefeated, the beast of the arena—and lost.

Bartise, glaring down at the scene, clenched his jaws and balled his fists tight. This wasn't how it was supposed to go. He had seen Wild Child run through opponents like they were nothing, but the impossible had happened now. The golden boy had fallen, and Bartise had no choice but to swallow the bitter pill that came with it.

With a deep, begrudging breath, Bartise stepped into the arena, wearing a mask of controlled fury. He took the microphone from Purp and forced out the words.

"The winner of tonight's competition," he paused, the words seeming to catch in his throat, "and the $5,000,000... ladies and gentlemen, Bloody Knuckles!"

There was no enthusiasm, or congratulatory tone in Bartise's voice. His announcement was more of a formality, something he was compelled to do despite the obvious pain it caused him. His eyes flickered to Wild Child on the ground, and for a brief moment, a flash of something like regret crossed his face. But it was gone as quickly as it appeared, replaced by a hard, steely gaze.

Bartise locked eyes with Bag Man and his anger soared to greater heights. When he saw him at the Jayvon and Hamza fight, he thought he knew him from somewhere but he didn't know where. But now that he'd cut off his dreadlocks and trimmed his beard, he knew exactly where he knew his ass from. Instantly, he was snapped back to the night Bag Man fucked him over.

CHAPTER SEVENTEEN

Oneida Correctional Facility was once a place for so-called rehabilitation, but now it functioned as something entirely different. The space was now used as an arena for street fighters. Every weekend fighters from all over the state of New York would come out to brawl for large amounts of cash. Pimps, players, thugs, hustlers, gangstas, and everybody who was anybody in the underworld would attend the epic sports event placing bets on the knockout kings they favored to win. The winner of the competition, if he or she was lucky, would walk away ten thousand dollars richer.

Every tier inside the correctional facility was packed with spectators clutching handfuls of money and egging on the fight taking place below. In addition to the people on the tier, there were some on the floor, encircling the two brawling men. Not only were they clutching dollars, but some of them were smoking, drinking, and/or doing drugs.

The atmosphere was humid. It also smelled of blood, sweat, mold, and urine. The floor was completely covered in blood-stained cardboard, bodily secretions, fingernails, and broken teeth. This place had seen many battles as well as many deaths, when it was up and running, and even now that it was shut down.

Come on. We're gonna have to sell this thing if you want the crowd to buy it, Bag Man thought as he threw two jabs at Napalm and then a right cross. His punches knocked his head backward and sent sweat flying. Bag Man was a six-foot-one cat with a brown hue, an unkempt beard, and long hair he kept in box braids. He had a lean muscular physique that was a true testament to his ghetto workouts. His attire was a wife beater, camouflage cargo pants, and construction Timbs.

"Come on. Bring it!" Bag Man yelled at Napalm and motioned for him to come on. Napalm, a Vietnamese man with a braided ponytail hanging to his ass and was built like a fucking superhero, shook off his daze and charged Bag Man like he was a matador. He threw haymakers at Bag Man trying to knock his head off. Xavier, with his superhuman reflexes, avoided the six-foot-four man's attack easily.

This son of a bitch's punches pack one hell of a wallop. I done took a few blows from 'em to make this shit look good. I may not feel it now, but inna A.M. a nigga gon' be aching. That's for damn sure, Bag Man thought about the next assault Napalm would launch against him. *He'd started fighting in the underground circuit so he'd be able to keep paying for his wife, Valentina's stomach cancer treatments while she was laid up in the hospital. The loot he made delivering packages for UPS and selling weed on the side wasn't shit but a drop in the bucket when it came to all the expenses he was responsible for. So when he'd heard about the bag a brawler could make at the underground fighting tournament 'Hell', he jumped at the opportunity to participate.* Bag Man had spent six months of weekends as the Knockout King and had developed an impeccable reputation.

Napalm laid into Bag Man with body shots and made his face ball up in pain. He then gave him a left to his abs and followed up with an uppercut. The blow sent him stumbling back hastily. He bounced off a dirty mattress tied around one of many pillars on the ground floor. When he peeled his eyes open, Napalm came charging at him like a raging primate. He unleashed a flurry of punches to his body and several more to his head. His fists felt like twenty-pound boxing gloves against Isaiah's head and body. The impact of every headshot sent a mixture of sweat and blood flying in every direction. Isaiah's eyes were rolled to the back of his head and his bloody mouth was hanging open. He was under a dizzy spell from the merciless beating he was getting.

This bitch 'pose to be pulling his punches but he's coming at me with all he's got. The fuck? He's tryna take my head off, Bag Man thought as he stumbled backward in a hurry. He righted his footing before he could meet the ground, spat blood, and threw his fists back up. He stole a glance in the direction of Bartise who'd promised him five times the amount of money he'd get if he purposely lost the fight. If he followed through with their agreement then he stood to walk away with 100 bandz. That kind of money would help to pay a hefty sum for his wife's medical treatment so he was counting on it.

Bartise was wearing a Gucci headband, matching sweatshirt and sneakers. He occasionally puffed on a fat ass blunt of Ganja wedged between his thick fingers and blew out smoke clouds. He was posted up beside that nigga, Purp. Purp's swarthy pigmentation, coupled with his usual dark attire, camouflaged him perfectly in the shadows.

Napalm's fists were lightning fast and Bag Man moved just as quickly, ducking and dodging them. He slipped behind his opponent and put his big ass in a full Nelson. Napalm's face balled up and he gritted, struggling to get out of the hold Bag Man had placed him in.

"What the fuck are you doing, bitch? You're supposed to pull the punches, asshole." Bag Man told him as sweat and blood trickled down his face.

"There will be a snow fight in hell the day I take orders from a fucking chimp! I don't need you to take a fall; I can beat chu straight up." Napalm said with a strained voice, trying to break Bag Man's hold.

"Oh, yeah?" Bag Man asked through gritted teeth, tightening his hold and dripping sweat on him.

"Y—yeah!" Napalm replied and grabbed a handful of Bag Man jewels. He squeezed them as hard as he could. Bag Man's eyes became as big as golf balls and he hollered out in excruciation. As soon as he released Napalm, he turned around and grabbed the front of his wife beater. Grunting, he lifted him and threw his ass across the room. Bag Man Rocketed through the air and slammed into a cell door. The impact sent dust flying from it and cockroaches emerged from the cracks and crevasses of it. Bag Man landed hard on his back and fell to the side. He lay on the floor balled up with a pained expression and holding his aching side. He slowly picked his throbbing head up from the ground. When he looked ahead he had blurred vision and was seeing double so he shook the cobwebs from his head. His vision came into focus and he looked up at Napalm. He was holding both his fists up in the air and wolfing big shit while turning around in a 360-degree turn.

"Yeaaah, this guy's nothing! Nothing! What good is a man against a beast?" Napalm shouted out at the surrounding audience. They were hooting, hollering, and egging him to finish Bag Manoff. "I'll let chu decide, shall I finish him off now, or take my time?" he held up his thick calloused thumb, turning it up and down to get the audience's answer. They all held up their thumbs and then pointed them down. "The people have spoken so now I must break you in halves!" Napalm smiled sinisterly and turned around to Xavier. He was down on one knee holding his side. He winced now and again with blood dripping from his chin.

Napalm made his way over to the metal tabletop and began climbing upon it. Bag Man looked at Bartise and he was looking at him while whispering something to Purp. He then looked around at all the people in attendance. Most of them were chanting Napalm's name and pumping fistfuls of money in the air. With his downfall came a lot of money for them, and the idea of them being happy, fucked with his soul. He whipped his head to Napalm who was still smiling sinisterly. The arrogant bastard was even throwing his hands up and down, hyping up the crowd before he gave them the finish they were hungry for.

Furious, Bag Man scrambled to his boots and charged at Napalm. When Napalm turned around his eyes bulged seeing Bag Man leaping into the air. Before he could make a move, Bag Man's booted feet crashed into him with the force of a cannonball. Bag Man landed on the tabletop while Napalm rocketed across the room and slammed high up against a pillar. The impact rocked *the pillar and debris trickled from the ceiling. Napalm flailed his arms and legs as he hurled back towards the ground. His neck banged off the edge of a table below and he landed face up. He winced and hollered out.*

"Christ, I—I—I can't move my arms and legs!" Napalm complained teary-eyed. The thought of being a quadriplegic terrified him.

The spectators were still in an uproar while the referee, a short white dude with a shiny bald head, walked over to examine Napalm. Bag Man hopped off the table top still holding his side. He looked at Bartise who mad dogged him then set his sights on the referee and waited for him to deliver the verdict.

CHAPTER EIGHTEEN

Please, let this fool be able to fight. I don't need this crazy nigga after my ass. More importantly, I need this bread for Valentina's treatments, Bag Man thought with a thudding heart. He could hear every beat within his ears and his palms were beginning to sweat.

The referee plucked an ink pen from his breast pocket. He poked Napalm at the bottoms of his feet, legs, torso, and palms and asked him if he could feel anything. The answer was no. The only place he had any feeling was his face and ears. Realizing his worst fear had come true; Napalm started crying like a newborn baby with snot bubbles coming out of his nostrils. The referee rose to his feet tucking his ink pen back into his breast pocket.

"Napalm is no longer able to continue the fight. So our winner this evening is the Ex-mannnnnnn!" The referee switched hands with the microphone he was speaking into and pointed at

Xavier. He then congratulated Bag Man and held his hand in the air by his wrist.

Bag Man locked eyes with Bartise while the referee held his hand in the air. The kingpin was staring at him with such intensity he thought he'd burst into blood, guts, and chunks of meat. It was then that he knew he and his wife were in grave danger. He had to get to her as quickly as possible if they hoped to escape The Big Apple with their lives. Keeping his eyes on Xavier, Bartise pulled his cellphone out of his suit's jacket and speed-dialed someone.

Bag Man snatched his hand from the referee and snatched up his motorcycle helmet, and black leather motorcycle jacket. He slipped them both on as he made hurried footsteps through the exit and made a right down the hallway. At this time, Bartise put away his cellular and tapped Purp's arm. Purp, toting a duffle bag full of dead presidents, walked over to Mr. Happy and his two Chinese bodyguards. Mr. Happy was a five-foot-five Chinese man with long silky black hair tied off by a red ribbon. His face was painted white; he wore eyeliner, red diamonds painted on his cheeks, red lipstick, and a hideous scar on either side of his mouth, shaped to form a smile. He wore a Dragons Qing Dynasty Emperor Tang Cap and a traditional Kimono Hanfu Cardigan Cloak.

One of Mr. Happy's bodyguards took the heavy duffle bag and slipped its strap over his shoulder. Mr. Happy smiled at Bartise and Purp, exchanging bows with them. With that, he motioned for his bodyguards to follow him as he headed for the exit.

"Lucky, tight-eyed muthafucka," Purp said under his breath as Mr. Happy, his bodyguards, and the audience spilled out of the exit. Bartise and Purp were the only ones left with an immobilized Napalm. He was lying in the same place on the floor as he was when the referee announced him out of the fight.

"Please, help—help me. C—call—an ambulance. Don't—don't leave me here." Napalm pleaded, looking in Bartise and Purp's direction. He watched as Bartise whispered something to Purp. The big baldhead nigga nodded and walked towards Napalm pulling out his handkerchief. He flapped the handkerchief open and held it down at his side. Napalm's eyes widened fearfully and he began to worry. "Wait a minute! What—what're you doing?" he tried to get up from the ground but his body wouldn't cooperate.

"Shhhhhhhhh." Purp shushed him with his finger to his lips as he kneeled beside Napalm.

"Bartise, please, don't allow him to do—" Napalm's words were cut short when Purp held his handkerchief over his nose and mouth with both hands. Napalm whipped his head from left to right trying his best to escape the huge man's iron-like hold.

"I'm sorry, kid. But if you go to the hospital then the cops are gonna show up asking questions. They're gonna show up asking questions that I'm not too sure you can keep your mouth shut about." Bartise told him from where he was posted up across the room.

Napalm stared up at Purp with teary eyes struggling to breathe, as the fight began to leave his body. Purp stared down at him with unforgiving eyes. He watched his eyelids flutter like the wings of a dying butterfly as his life force slowly left his body. A moment later, Napalm's eyes rolled up to their corners and he gave his last breath. Purp touched the pulse in his neck to confirm his death. He then stood upright refolding his handkerchief, kissing the gold cross hanging around his neck, and crossed himself in the sign of the holy crucifix. Purp took the time to admire his handiwork before tucking his handkerchief inside his breast pocket. Bartise patted him on his back and told him to let go before heading for the exit.

***

Bag Man ran as fast as he could out of the prison past spectators coming into the parking lot and leaving in their cars. He stuffed the last two stacks of his winnings inside the black leather pouch attached to his belt loops, zipped it up, and pulled out the keys to his Ducati Super Sport. He fired up the motorcycle, kicked up the kick-stand with the heel of his boot, and revved that bitch up. The bike whined loud and angrily and he zipped out of the parking lot, passing other whips leaving the prison's grounds.

Bartise and Purp stood outside his cloud-white Maybach 62 with pitch-black windows. They watched the lights of Bag Man's motorcycle disappear into the night before hopping inside the $350,000 luxury vehicle and leaving the scene.

***

Meanwhile

Bag Man was flying like a bat out of hell through the streets, covering block after block, passing cars on either side of him. He popped a wheelie, leaving the back end of his motorcycle on the asphalt. He brought his Ducati back down and took off even faster.

Debris went up in the air as the motorcycle whipped past an intersection, narrowly missing oncoming motorists. Drivers hurled vulgarities out of their windows and blew their horns furiously. Bag Man ignored them as he jumped in and out of lanes. He was going so fast that he came dangerously close to side-swiping nearby vehicles. He hit a couple of sharp turns and almost struck a few pedestrians before he reached his crib in Southside Jamaica, Queens.

Bag Man lowered his kickstand, turned off his motorcycle, and hopped off. He removed his motorcycle helmet and looked up at his house. When he saw the door was cracked open his heart skipped a beat and he panicked. Holding the helmet, he hurried up the steps and snatched the door open. Running inside, he slipped on something and went up in the air. He hit the floor hard, wincing, still holding his helmet. Feeling something wet on his hand, he looked at it, it was bloody. His eyes bucked and he thought of the worst. Seeing something in the corner of his eye, he looked beside him and found Valentina. Her eyes were stretched open, her mouth was ajar, and a hunting knife was standing up in her chest.

Bag Man's eyes filled up with tears seeing the love of his life laid out dead. He made an ugly face as he crawled towards her in a pool of blood.

"No, no, no, no, dear God, don't let it be her." Bag Man pleaded as tears slid down his cheeks. "Don't let it be my baby. My hummingbird, my sweet, sweet, darling Valentina." His voice cracked as he was attacked with a wave of emotions. His cheeks became drenched and snot peeked out of his right nostril. He scooted beside Valentina and pulled her into his arms, laying her head inside his lap. He pulled the knife out of her chest and tossed it aside. Then he swept her eyes closed and kissed her tenderly on her lips and forehead. "I'm so sorry, baby, I'm so sorry I wasn't here to save you. But I promise you. I promise you I'm gonna get those bastards that did this to you." He snarled and slammed his fist down on the floor. He then looked back down at Valentina caressing her bald head. She'd shaved her long black curly hair off once she'd begun losing it to chemotherapy. She was a *beautiful woman who was thick in all of the right places. But the fifty pounds she'd lost due to the cancer made her look like she was eighty pounds, soaking wet. Bag Man made sure she knew how beautiful she was and went out of his way to make her feel special. He brought her the most incredibly gorgeous bouquet of Lily flowers every day. He'd picked them personally from the garden she'd been working on in their backyard. He catered to her wants, needs, and all the extras. Valentina didn't have to lift a finger. She'd always felt loved by her husband and thought he couldn't do any more for her to be more in love with him than she already was. But she was wrong! In her time of need, Bag Man leveled up and made her fall deeper in love with him than she had ever been before.*

CHAPTER NINETEEN

Bartise's face contorted in rage, like an angry lion. "You," he spat, jumping off his throne and drawing his cobra head cane, revealing a hidden katana. "I'm gonna cut you into slices of salami," Bartise swore, taking swipes at Bag Man.

Bag Man ducked and dodged the blade with superhuman agility. His eyes darted around for something to defend himself with when he heard Chyna call out. He looked in Chyna's direction and the young nigga tossed his bamboo staff. Bag Man snatched it out of the air and drew its hidden katana. The sword's blade gleamed under the outside lighting.

The two men clashed, their katanas sending sparks flying. The sharp clangs of steel against steel echoed in the night. Both men ended up bleeding from cuts on their bodies, but it was Bartise who had taken the worst of it. His white suit was now crimson, soaked with his blood. Sweat poured down his face, and he grew pale from blood loss. His sword swings became slower and less precise.

Bag Man, noticing Bartise's weakening state, pressed his advantage. Bartise saw blurred images of Bag Man, who was smiling wickedly. With a final, desperate thrust, Bartise aimed his sword at Bag Man's heart, but Bag Man sidestepped, slicing Bartise across the kneecap and dropping him to one leg.

Bag Man then sliced off Bartise's thumb, making him drop his katana with a cry of pain. Seeing an opening to end the fight, Bag Man drove his blade through Bartise's chest and kicked him off his sword. Bartise collided with the ground, gasping for breath, life slowly fading.

Bag Man, glassy-eyed, looked up at the sky where the love of his life, Valentina resided. "You can finally rest in peace now, baby."

The crowd was silent, the tension dissipating as Bartise lay defeated. Jayvon, Chrissy, Chyna, and Augustus approached Bag Man, their expressions a mix of relief and admiration.

"You straight, G?" Jayvon asked, placing a hand on Bag Man's shoulder.

Bag Man, eyes still fixed on the sky, nodded. "She can rest now."

"Who?" Chyna frowned.

Bag Man looked at him. "My wife…Valentina."

Jayvon frowned. "Wait…you're the X-Man? The fighter that just up and—"

"Vanished?" Bag Man cut him short. "Yeah. That's me."

"Man, who woulda thought you'd been living right under our noses this whole time?" Chyna chimed in.

"Yep. You bitchez never even hadda cl—" Bag Man was interrupted by an animalistic roar behind him.

Bartise sprang back up with his katana, lunging at Bag Man with a crazed look in his eyes. Bag Man barely had time to duck out of the way before Bartise took a swipe at him. Completely missing Bag Man on the first try, Bartise went to bring his blade around and take another swipe at him. But before his sword could make contact, Delroy moved swiftly, drawing a gun made out of plastic. The weapon, silent but deadly, spat out a full clip of plastic projectiles into Bartise's chest. Bartise made the ugliest face stumbling back, his body jerking violently with each impact. Still holding his cobra head cane, he crashed to the ground, pain written across his face. With his last breath, Bartise pressed the hidden button on his cane. The last thing he saw before the lights in his eyes dimmed was Bag Man's scowling face.

The ground rumbled loudly and hidden doors slid open. An army of intelligent chimps emerged from the depths of hidden tunnels. They wore bulletproof vests and were armed with M-16s.

They moved coordinated as they flooded the arena and turned it into a battlefield.

Jayvon and Neo exchanged glances, acknowledging what had to be done. They dove into the fray, fighting side by side, their blows synchronized like swimmers as they took out chimp after chimp.

Chyna and Bag Man weren't far behind. Chyna moved with lethal grace, his fists and feet a blur as he struck with pinpoint accuracy. Bag Man, still amped from the Bartise fight, took down chimps with powerful, bone-crunching blows.

Luka, LaDecia, and their offspring drew non-metallic knives, ceramic blades, and other weapons they snuck in through the detectors. They went at the chimps, slicing, cutting, kicking, and punching them. The beasts' blood sprayed their faces and clothes, but they ignored the mess. They grabbed the M-16s of the fallen animals and started firing at those still in the fight.

Neo locked his arms around a chimp's neck and brutally snapped it, killing the beast instantly. It dawned on him that he hadn't seen McGuiness. He frantically scanned the grounds for him and found him being torn apart and eaten by chimps. At the corner of his eye, he saw Jayvon having a tough time trying to fight off two chimps. So he picked up a M-16 and sprayed them both. Breathing heavily, Jayvon grinned and saluted him. Neo returned the gesture.

Despite the chimps' numbers and firepower, they weren't any match for the sheer ferocity of Jayvon and company.

But the tide was turning. More chimps kept pouring out of the tunnels, in overwhelming numbers. The air was filled with the roar of gunfire, the screams of the wounded, and the chaos of battle. The situation was spiraling out of control, and everyone knew it.

"We needa get the hell outta here!" Jayvon shouted to Neo, chopping down another chimp as he fought his way towards the exit.

The crowd surged toward the only visible way out, but their hopes were dashed when they saw the steel-bar shutter slam down, trapping them inside. Bartise's security guards, loyal to the end, had locked the exit to contain the situation. As the guests pounded on the shutter in panic, the guards climbed into two black Jeep Wranglers and sped off, leaving the arena in dust.

Shit, Neo thought, seeing the steel-bars coming down. "If we're gonna get outta here then we're gonna have to get those bars up," he told Jayvon.

"Right," Jayvon replied.

"Ma! Dad! Delroy! Jayvon and I are gonna try to lift those bars, cover us." Neo shouted.

Luka, LaDecia, Chyna, Bag Man, Delroy, and the rest of the survivors formed a defensive line. They sprayed the advancing chimps. Empty shell casings flew over their shoulders as flames burst from their assault rifles. Bullets whizzed past their heads, and shoulders, coming dangerously close to ending their lives. With the cover fire in full effect, Jayvon and Neo ran to the steel-bar shutter and attempted to lift it. Sweat bubbled on their foreheads. They gritted. Veins bulged on their necks and arms as the steel-bars slowly began to rise. Juggernaut Jones, King Smite, and the rest of the fighters raced over to help them. The steel-bars rose further and further until it was enough space for everyone to get out. Jayvon and Neo held the steel-bars for everyone to exit.

The crowd scrambled out into the night air, desperate to escape the hellish scene behind them.

Once they were outside, they scattered in every direction, racing to their cars. They fired up their engines and peeled out, putting as much distance between themselves and the nightmare inside the arena.

Jayvon and Neo looked over their shoulders, Luka and the gang were running their way. With every moment that past the steel-bar shutter seemed to grow heavier and heavier, making them crouch lower to the asphalt.

"Hurry! This shit is not getting any lighter," Jayvon strained, face balling up.

"He has a point." Neo strained, face balling as well. Both men looked like they were trying to deadlift the heaviest weights of their lives.

Jayvon and Neo were the last to exit, dropping the steel-bar shutter with a loud crash.

***

Shorty groaned as a skinny, white chick in a purple wig and soccer ball-sized breasts rode him like a wild horse, digging her acrylic nails into his hairy chest, her facial features twisting into a parade of sex faces. Shorty's cellphone vibrated and danced across the nightstand, but he was too wrapped up in the moment to give a fuck. The cellphone rang over and over again, seemingly insisting he answered it.

"I gotta get that. It may be important," Shorty said, his head sinking back into the pillow, eyes narrowing into slits.

"Just let it ring, I'm almost there," she moaned, her eyes rolling back and her mouth hanging open. She rode him so fast and hard that the bed springs squeaked in a frantic rhythm.

The cellphone stopped ringing and then started back up again.

"I really gotta see who this is," he insisted, irritation creeping into his voice.

"Oh, Jesus, I'm so close!" she groaned, her face contorted like a masked killer was coming at her.

Without warning, Shorty shoved her off him and she thudded against the floor. The white chick stared up at him, stunned and furious. She quickly slipped into her thong and yanked on the rest of her clothes.

"I don't know who the fuck you think you are, but no one treats me like that, you fucking prick," she ranted, grabbing her pocketbook and storming to the door.

Shorty watched as she slammed the door with so much force it shook the walls. He thought about chasing after her and smacking her for the disrespect—but his attention shifted back to his phone, his eyes catching a missed call from Draco.

He knew this call was critical, so he hit him back with the quickness.

"What's up, bro?" Shorty asked, sitting up in bed. "Say less." he hung up and then hit up his right-hand. "Giggles, I just got that call," Shorty said, his voice hardening as he adjusted the phone against his ear. "Get the soldados together. I'll be there in thirty." He hung up and began getting dressed for the night's mission.

Draco hadn't received his other portion of the money so he put the greenlight on Jayvon and his family. He had appointed a kill-squad headed by Shorty for the mission. Under the little nigga's leadership, he was positive they'd execute his orders without a hitch.

CHAPTER TWENTY

Shorty wasn't taking any chances. Rumors about Jayvon's crew were enough to make him bring backup—three of his best hitters. Each of them wore sinister clown masks, with faces painted in twisted grins that belied the deadly intent behind them. Moving like shadows, they scaled the fences with practiced ease, their boots didn't make a sound as they landed on the other side.

They fanned out across the property, their movements precise and coordinated. They were here for one reason: to execute everyone in that bitch. The night air was thick with tension, and as the masked men advanced, they knew they were ready for whatever—or whoever—came their way.

***

Chrissy and Augustus lounged on the living room couch, the comforting glow of the television filling the room as they devoured slices of pizza and watched a rerun of *The Boys*. For once, the world outside felt distant, like it couldn't reach them in this little bubble of peace.

"I'll be back," Augustus grunted, using one of his crutches to hoist himself off the couch.

Chrissy glanced over, one eyebrow raised. "Where are you going?"

Augustus paused in the doorway, a crooked smile on his face. "To take a shit, lil' lady."

Chrissy scrunched her nose in mock disgust. "Ewww, you could've kept that info to yourself."

As Augustus shuffled away, his laughter echoed down the hallway. Chrissy shook her head, a smirk tugging at her lips. "That's what yo' ass gets for being nosey!" Augustus hollered, voice fading as he moved farther away.

Chrissy chuckled, making her way to the kitchen. She opened the fridge, her eyes darting over the contents. "My God, I'm having pregnancy cravings already? Why do I suddenly want pickles with peanut butter and sardines?"

But she didn't notice the front door quietly swinging open behind her. Two of Shorty's hitters slipped inside like shadows, their faces masked and eyes gleaming with malice. They moved with the quiet precision of wolves, stalking their prey, weapons at the ready, eager to unleash violence.

The lead hitter, Giggles, crept toward the kitchen, his gun raised, eyes locked on Chrissy's back. The plan was simple: eliminate anyone inside. But he had no idea who he was dealing with.

Chrissy's instincts flared. She whipped around just as he crossed the threshold with a gleam of steel in her hand—a pistol-grip, pump-action shotgun. The muzzle gleamed under the kitchen light like a predator's tooth.

Bloom!

The shotgun roared like a jaguar unleashed. The blast was deafening. Giggles was lifted off his feet and slammed against the wall. His body crumpled to the floor like a ragdoll and left a smear of blood behind.

Before his partner could react, Chrissy pumped the shotgun again.

Bloom!

Another thunderous explosion rocked the room. The second hitter staggered backward, his gun clattering to the floor as his body hit the surface with a sickening thud. The kitchen, once filled with the warmth of everyday life, was now a blood-soaked battlefield.

Silence fell, broken only by the hum of the refrigerator and the faint, rhythmic tapping of Augustus's crutches in the hallway. Chrissy's breath came in sharp, uneven gasps, her heart pounding like a war drum. She hadn't just defended herself; she had survived. But it wasn't over yet.

Augustus appeared in the doorway, his eyes widening in shock. "Chrissy, what the hell happened?"

"They came in through the front door," she said, voice steadier than she felt. "I don't know how many more there are. We need to secure the house."

She felt a fierce surge of protectiveness, thinking of the life growing inside her. Her gaze darted to Augustus, who was standing, frozen, his expression a mix of shock and awe. Before she could ask why he hadn't moved to retrieve a weapon, two more men in clown masks appeared on either side of him, guns drawn.

"This shit ain't gonna go the way you think, mami," one of them snarled. "I suggest you drop that piece before we leave this old black mothafucka all over this nice living room you got here."

Chrissy hesitated, her finger twitching on the trigger. The other man in the clown mask sneered. "Drop the shotgun, bitch! We're not playin' games with you!"

Augustus's voice cut through the tension. "Chrissy, you drop that piece and these spics are gonna do me and you," he warned. "This was a sanctioned hit. These are Draco's—"

He was cut short by a swift blow to the back of the head from Shorty's hitter. Augustus crumpled to the floor but managed to use one of his crutches to knock Shorty's gun away. As the hitter aimed to finish him off, Chrissy acted on instinct, leveling the shotgun.

Bloom!

The blast sent the hitter flying, one of his sneakers left behind where he'd stood. Shorty, heart thundering in his chest, stared at her with wide, terrified eyes. He opened his mouth to scream, but Chrissy's shotgun roared again.

Shorty's body slammed into the wall, leaving a deep dent before collapsing lifelessly onto the floor.

Chrissy didn't waste a second. She switched the shotgun to her other hand and rushed to Augustus, pulling him to his feet. He glanced around at the carnage, eyes wide. "Remind me to always stay on your good side, young lady," he muttered.

Chrissy grinned, relief flooding her veins as she hugged him tight. "I better call 911, and then Von."

Augustus, catching his breath, managed a wry smile. "While you're doin' that, I'll be in the kitchen makin' myself a drink," he said, hobbling toward the fridge on his crutches. "God knows I need one. That was one hell of a close call."

***

Purp and Stutter-Box wore stone faces as they stood over Bartise's body. The once feared and untouchable kingpin now lay cold on the marble floor, his chest riddled with plastic bullets.

Purp knelt down and gently closed Bartise's eyes, the weight of the moment pressing heavily on his shoulders. Stutter-Box followed, carefully draping his jacket over Bartise's corpse, in a silent gesture of respect.

In unison, the two men crossed themselves, the ritual bringing a fleeting sense of peace amidst the turmoil. But that peace was quickly replaced by a burning resolve. Purp's hand clenched into a fist as he stood back up, his voice low and deadly. "We're gonna make them pay for this," he swore, the promise thick with vengeance.

Stutter-Box nodded, "Let's get these muthafuckaz, bro." He spoke without stammering for the first time, grim determination dripping from his vocal cords. He took an M-16 assault rifle from a dead monkey's hands and checked its clip. It was nearly full. There was no need for words; Bartise's boys knew what had to be done.

Purp swung his leg over his Ducati Super Sport, pressed the start button, and brought the sleek black machine back to life. Stutter-Box climbed on behind, securing his arms around Purp as he revved the engine. They sped away from the mansion, the tires screeching as they went through a secret passage only Bartise and they knew about, the battlegrounds growing smaller and smaller behind them.

As they raced toward the parking lot where the survivors had scattered, Purp's mind was laser-focused. Bartise's death wouldn't go unanswered. There would be blood, and they'd hunt down every last person involved.

"There they are!" Stutter-Box pointed out Bag Man and everyone he'd fled with. Purp scowled and clenched his jaws, revving the Ducati before taking off. The motorcycle was a blur of speed and fury. Purp and Stutter-Box were prepared to unleash their wrath.

Steering the bike with one hand, Purp upped his gun with the other, squeezing the trigger relentlessly.

Boc! Boc! Boc! Boc! Boc!

Bag Man, Jayvon, Chyna, Neo, and everyone else scattered like roaches when the lights came on in a project apartment.

Bag Man and the gang dove behind parked cars. The air was heavy with the smell of gunpowder and the deafening roar of gunfire. Shards of glass and twisted metal flew like deadly confetti, the relentless barrage tearing through everything in its path. Purp swung the Ducati around with a growl, parking it with a practiced ease. As he reloaded his gun, Stutter-Box took over, the M-16 roaring as it spat out round after round. Bullets ripped through car hoods, shredded tires, and sent windshields exploding in showers of glass. The once-pristine rides sagged under the onslaught, now nothing more than bullet-riddled wrecks.

Purp reloaded and ready, hopped off the bike, his eyes locked on his targets. This was it—time to make them pay for Bartise's death. But as he moved in, Delroy popped up from behind cover, busting his gun. A bullet tore into Purp's shoulder, spinning him around and sending him crashing to the pavement. Purp gritted his teeth, crawling away, leaving a trail of blood in his wake. Delroy, adrenaline pumping, barked at Luka and LaDecia to stay down as he prepared to finish off Purp. But before he could make his move, Stutter-Box sent a hail of bullets his way, forcing Delroy to duck back behind cover.

Suddenly, the relentless gunfire ceased—the M-16's clip had run dry. Stutter-Box cursed under his breath, fumbling to reload, but realized he was out of ammo. That's when Neo struck, flying at Stutter-Box in a blur of fury, his foot connected with the man's jaw in a bone-crunching kick. Stutter-Box went down hard, hitting the pavement with a sickening thud. He tried to shake off the blow, but before he could gather his senses, Jayvon appeared out of nowhere, delivering a brutal kick to his forehead. The impact snapped his head back against the asphalt. Blood poured from the wound, his eyes glazing over with confusion and pain.

Jayvon and Neo didn't give him a chance to recover. They descended on him like hungry hyenas, their feet slamming into his body with unrelenting fury. Stutter-Box's feeble attempts to shield himself were met with even more vicious kicks, each driving him further into the pavement. Chyna and Bag Man joined in, their faces twisted with rage, their kicks and stomps fueled by a desire for revenge. The four of them pounded Stutter-Box into oblivion, their blows turning his face into a pulpy mess, unrecognizable beneath the blood and broken bone.

When they finally stepped back, breathing hard, Stutter-Box was nothing more than a lifeless heap, his body broken and beaten beyond repair. The parking lot was eerily quiet, the drama momentarily subdued, as they stood over his mangled corpse. It wasn't just a victory it was a statement—a brutal reminder that no one fucked with them and lived to tell the tale.

CHAPTER TWENTY-ONE

Purp peeked out from behind the car he'd ducked behind and saw Stutter-Box lying dead on the ground. Jayvon, Neo, Bag Man, and Chyna stood over the body, breathing hard, their faces smeared with blood and sweat.

"Damn, Stutter," Purp muttered, feeling a twist of anger and sorrow. He checked his clip, preparing to launch one last attack. Just as he was about to squeeze the trigger, LaDecia came out of nowhere, her foot smashing into the side of his head.

Purp's skull cracked against the passenger window, the glass spider-webbing from the impact. He hit the pavement hard, his gun clattering out of reach. Wincing, he touched the back of his head, feeling the warm, sticky blood on his fingers. He scrambled to grab his gun, but a heavy foot stomped down on his hand, pinning it to the ground. Purp looked up, squinting through the pain, and saw Luka towering over him, his face twisted in an undying hatred.

"The big dogs have eaten already," Luka growled, his voice low and menacing. "I think it's time we let our pups eat. What do you say, lovey?" He reached out and grasped LaDecia's hand.

"Yes. I believe our pups are very hungry," LaDecia replied, a chilling smile spreading across her face.

Luka kissed her hand softly and they took a step back.

Their kids—except for Neo—descended on Purp like a pack of wolves. Punches and kicks rained down on him from every direction, each blow more vicious than the last. Purp tried to shield himself, but there was no escaping the brutal onslaught. By the time they were done, Purp was barely recognizable. His face was swollen and bloody and his body was broken.

Jayvon, catching his breath after the brutal takedown of Purp and Stutter-Box, felt his cellphone ringing in his pocket. He pulled it out, seeing an incoming FaceTime call from Chrissy. He quickly answered, and her familiar face filled the screen, calm and composed.

"Hey, baby," she greeted, her voice steady.

Jayvon's brow furrowed with concern. "What's up, Doll? You good?"

"Yeah, I'm fine," she replied, her tone almost casual. "Some men in clown masks broke into the house, and tried to kill me and Augustus."

Jayvon's heart skipped a beat. "What? Are you hurt? Where's Augustus?"

"We're both okay, babe," she reassured him. "We fought them off. Twelve just left after taking our report. Augustus and I are cleaning up the mess now."

Jayvon exhaled, the tension in his chest easing slightly. "I'm coming back on the first flight I can get. I swear."

Chrissy smiled softly. "We're fine, Jay. Just hurry back when you can."

"I love you, ma," Jayvon said, his voice full of sincerity.

"I love you too, Baby," she responded. "Tell the boys I love them also."

"Most def," Jayvon nodded. "I gotta lotta shit to tell you about this trip when we get back."

Chrissy smiled. "I can imagine," she blew him a kiss.

As the call ended, Jayvon exchanged a look with Chyna, then glanced at Bag Man and the others. "Let's roll," he said.

They moved quickly, piling into two separate stretch Lincoln Navigators. Just as they were about to pull off, a Lincoln Navigator cruised past them. They pulled out behind it, and in the rearview mirror, Jayvon saw another stretch Navigator following, carrying Luka, LaDecia, Delroy, Wild Child, and four of their kids. The convoy moved as one, cutting through the night, leaving behind the carnage and the bodies of those who dared to try them.

***

"You're gonna have to step on it, mamas, before we lose them," Finesse said from the passenger seat, cocking his Glock. His date, the driver of the Navigator he'd rented during his stay in Bali, glanced at him, her eyes focused.

Shorty mashed the gas pedal, the engine roaring as they closed the distance between them and the stretch Navigator Jayvon was chauffeured in. The night air was filled with tension and the city lights seemed to flash by in a blur. Finesse smiled fiendishly and licked his lips. Reaching over, he held a button down and lowered the passenger window. The cold air rushed inside, ruffling his hair and clothes, but he didn't bat an eye. His eyes were locked on the driver's side of the stretch Navigator, his mind calculating his next move.

"Pull up to the driver's side," Finesse instructed, his voice thick with authority. He planned to take out the driver, leaving the passengers stranded and at his mercy. It would give him the advantage he needed to finish what he'd started.

***

As the cityscape blurred by, Finesse's mind flashed back to the parking lot at Bartise's place. It was there that he'd spotted Jayvon, barely noticing him at first. But then, in a brief moment, he'd caught sight of Chrissy's face on Jayvon's phone as they FaceTimed. Her voice, calling him "baby," had triggered something in Finesse. He'd pieced it together instantly—Jayvon was someone close to Chrissy.

Finesse had already suspected Jayvon might have been involved in jacking his safe house, but now he didn't care. Even if Jayvon wasn't the one, taking him out would still devastate Chrissy. And that was enough for Finesse. He was going to hurt her in the worst way possible, by taking away the one she cared about most—her man.

"Easy. Easy, ma," Finesse murmured, signaling his date to ease off the gas pedal. He scooted closer to the passenger door and eased his Glock out the window. With a steady hand, he squeezed the trigger twice.

Blocka! Blocka!

Finesse's brows furrowed as scratches appeared on the stretch Navigator's driver-side window. "What the fuck?" he muttered under his breath. "That muthafucka's bulletproof."

"What?" his date asked, glancing at him quickly.

"I said, the limousine's bulletproof!" Finesse snapped, slamming his fist against the window pane. Frustration tightened his jaw. "Yo, catch up with them. I'ma take out the front tire."

"Got it."

As their Navigator surged forward, Finesse hung halfway out of the window, his eyes laser-focused on the stretch Navigator's front tire. He was about to fire when the stretch Navigator suddenly swerved and slammed into the side of their vehicle. The impact sent Finesse's Navigator veering off course, jerking him violently in his seat and causing him to drop his gun. He nearly fell out of the window but managed to pull himself back inside, only to see a glaring light in the corner of his eye.

His heart plummeted as he turned to see a bus hurtling toward them, full speed ahead.

"Ooh, sh—"

Finesse's words were cut off as the bus collided with his Navigator and crushed its front end like an empty soda can. The force of the impact launched him out of the passenger window and sent him tumbling down the street at breakneck speed. He finally came to a stop, battered, bruised, and disoriented.

Struggling to gather his wits, Finesse looked up just in time to see a car speeding straight at him, the driver laying on the horn. He rolled out of the way, narrowly avoiding being hit, and exhaled a shaky breath of relief. But before he could fully catch his breath, another horn blared over his shoulder. He turned his head and his eyes widened in terror as another car sped toward him.

There was no time to react.

"Aaaaaaaaaaa—"

Boonk! Ba-donk! Boom!

The speeding car ran over Finesse and crushed him beneath its tires. Another car followed, then another, and then a third. When the street finally quieted, Finesse lay there—a bloody heap of flesh, once dressed in expensive clothes, now lifeless and mangled in the middle of the road.

***

Meanwhile

Further down the street, Finesse's rented Navigator was parked haphazardly amidst shattered glass and twisted wreckage. The once pristine vehicle now stood as a grim reminder of the chaos that had just unfolded. Drivers and passengers from other vehicles gathered, pulling out their cellphones, and capturing the gruesome aftermath. A few of them hit up the law and urgently relayed the details of the carnage.

The bus driver, who had been part of the accident, urged his passengers to stay onboard as he hopped down to the pavement. He pushed through the gathering crowd. His eyes widened in disbelief as he approached the wrecked Navigator. The mangled mess inside the truck hardly resembled something that had once been alive.

Finesse's date, who had been behind the wheel, was slumped forward, her lifeless body pinned by the steering wheel and crushed dashboard. Her eyes bulged grotesquely, her mouth hung open, and her entire face was a bloody, disfigured mess.

"Man, she looks like something outta the *Hellraiser* movie got her," a teenager in the crowd whispered, unable to tear his eyes away from the horrific scene.

***

"That's what I'm talking about, baby!" Jayvon's shouted as he and Chyna shook the driver's shoulder excitedly. The near miss with Finesse had everyone on edge, but now, relief washed over them.

Bag Man reached over, his massive hand colliding with the driver's in a solid dap, his grin wide and approving. The passengers—Luka and LaDecia's kids—clapped, their faces glowing with respect and admiration for the driver who had just saved their asses.

"Man, I can't believe that crazy ass nigga Finesse followed us out here," Chyna whispered in Jayvon's ear, his voice dripping disbelief and awe at the narrow escape.

"Maybe he didn't," Jayvon replied, leaning back into the plush leather seat, thinking. "There were a lotta rich niggaz out tonight. Could be he just happened to be one of 'em, just at the wrong time."

Chyna was about to respond when his cellphone rang, the screen lighting up with a FaceTime call. He gave the gesture for everyone in the limousine to be quiet. It was King Morpheus. This was it. The moment the young nigga had been waiting for.

Chyna accepted the call, and the faces of King Morpheus, King Shyne, and King Yak appeared, their expressions serious. This wasn't just a call—it was a coronation. The weight of the moment settled in. Chyna was about to be crowned the outside leader of the Kings of Thieves. This position carried not just authority, but the responsibility to command a vast and ruthless organization.

"Hold up K.O.T.," King Morpheus instructed, his voice steady and commanding. Chyna complied, his fingers forming the sign as he repeated the words of the oath. Jayvon, watching from the side, felt a chill run down his spine. This was more than just an initiation—it was history in the making.

As Chyna finished the oath, the founding members broke into applause, their faces lighting up with approval. King Morpheous leaned forward, his eyes locking onto Chyna's. "Welcome, King Chyna. You're now sitting inna seat of great power."

Chyna nodded, feeling the weight of the crown settle on his shoulders. Then came the question that sealed his fate as a leader:

"What's your first order of business as the free leader of the Kings of Thieves?"

CHAPTER TWENTY-TWO

Chyna didn't hesitate. He turned to Jayvon, who gave him a nod of encouragement, his eyes gleaming with pride. Then, with the calm authority of a man born to lead, Chyna gave his first command.

The founding members' faces darkened with satisfaction, their expressions mirroring the brutality that had built their empire. King Morpheus spoke last, his voice a low rumble. "Consider it done."

As the call ended, the gravity of the moment settled in the limousine. Jayvon had just taken his first step into the abyss of power, and there was no turning back. He wasn't just a member of the Kings of Thieves anymore—he was their leader on the outside, the man who would steer them into the future. And he'd just made it clear that under his rule, there would be no mercy for those who crossed him.

The limousine sped through the night, leaving behind the wreckage of Finesse's failed ambush, the sounds of the city fading as they moved closer to their next destination.

Inside, the air buzzed with anticipation and a newfound respect for the man who had just taken the helm of one of the most feared organizations in the underworld.

Bag Man, Luka, and LaDecia's kids congratulated Chyna. Jayvon threw his arm around his shoulders and kissed the side of his head.

There wasn't anything like brotherly love.

***

Once King Morpheus ended the FaceTime call with Chyna, his eyes narrowed with calculated intent. He turned to King Yak, his voice firm and direct.

"Yak, I need that situation handled immediately," Morpheus ordered, his tone leaving no room for delay.

King Yak nodded without hesitation, understanding the gravity of the command. "I'm onnit," he replied, moving towards the exit to handle the task.

Morpheus watched as Yak left the cell, knowing that once his orders were in motion, there would be no turning back. The Kings of Thieves were a well-oiled machine, and any threat to their reign would be dealt with swiftly and without mercy.

***

The alarm at the prison blared angrily and annoyingly. Most of the lights were out, but the small fires from burning mattresses, confetti, and toilet paper slithering from above kept most areas reasonably lit. The commodes overflowed out of nearly every cell, slicking their floors with water and soggy turds. The murky water rolled out onto the gallery and dripped off the edge, like rainwater. The entrances and exits of various locations of the facility were blocked by mattresses, office furniture, chairs, sofas, and anything else those held as prisoners could think of to act as a blockade.

Convicts and corrections officers alike decorated the grounds dead, some barely alive, moaning in excruciation. Far off in the distance the screams, hollers, shouts, and war cries of men bounced off the walls. Cars that were at odds behind the wall, noticeably the Puerto Ricans and the Kings of Thieves, were engaged in combat. There were smears of blood on the walls and the floors. The smell of death and bodily fluids made the air almost impossible to breathe without a gas mask or other facial covering.

There was a man's labored breathing, then the sounds of his hurried footsteps moving through the facility. The illumination of the various fires shone on him, casting his shadow on the jail's walls as he fled from what he believed was certain death.

DeMozzio huffed and puffed, wiping his sweaty forehead with the back of his bloody hand. His eyes were bucked, his mouth was hanging open, and his chest was heaving. His adrenaline was pumping like it was on steroids. He was terrified.

DeMozzio glanced over his shoulder for what had been the twentieth time in five minutes, hoping he wouldn't see his assailant still chasing him. Too bad for him, there Luger was, on his heels, holding a knife that was thirsty for another taste of his blood. "Oh, shit! Oh, shit!" he said in a panic, holding his wounded chest. He wiped the sweat from his forehead again, but this time he left a streak of blood behind.

"My G, this banga and I came seeking retribution for our comrade, and we're not leavin' until we claim it! My word to the crowns!" Luger swore with a balled-up face and flaring nostrils. His voice sounded demonic to DeMozzio. He was coming at him like a hungry jackal.

DeMozzio bent the corner and trampled through the toilet water, splashing it around. He looked over his shoulder and Luger was quickly closing the distance between them. He hurried up the slick steps that led to the top tier. Halfway up he lost his footing, and hurled forward, banging his forehead off one of the metal steps. He went crossed-eyed and saw double. Blood oozed out of his scalp, and slid down his face.

DeMozzio was dizzy, and his head was killing him. He blinked his eyes and looked around. Suddenly it hit him that Luger had been after him and he wasn't that far behind. That thought seemed to renew his stamina. He jumped back upon his sneakers and hurried up the steps, holding onto the guard rail. He ran down the gallery toward his cell. He intended on securing the extra poker he'd stashed for situations like this to defend himself. Once he'd gotten his hand on his seven inches of hard, sharp metal, he was sure that the tables would turn in his favor. Locking eyes with the open door of his cell, DeMozzio smiled joyfully. That smile turned into an expression of terror when he came within a few feet of his cell.

King Coopa appeared out of his cell like a magic trick wearing a prison-made stocking over his face, much like the one Luger had. He pulled a large piece of plexiglass from around his back. DeMozzio estimated it to be three inches thick and eight inches in length. King Coopa smiled sinisterly then scowled and squared his jaws.

"It's time you felt the wrath of the Kings!" King Coopa said with emphasis on the word "Kings", slamming the rigid plexiglass into DeMozzio and lifting him to the tips of his sneakers. DeMozzio's eyes stretched wide-open and blood poured out the corner of his mouth. He stared at King Coopa accusingly before trying to claw at his face. King Coopa turned his face away from his pathetic attempt to attack him. Grunting, he slammed the plexiglass into DeMozzio over and over again, each time harder than the last.

King Coopa yanked the plexiglass out of

DeMozzio, spun him around and wrapped his arm around his neck. DeMozzio struggled to get loose but the loss of blood left him weak. When he saw Luger standing before him, he already knew what time it was. He could only hope that his death would be quick.

King Coopa held DeMozzio in a place and Luger handed down the Death Blow. Without mercy, Luger butchered the poor son of a bitch. Stabbing him in his chest and torso over sixty times. Once Luger was finished with him, his face was sweaty, and his uniform was covered in dots of blood.

"This is what chu get when you fuck with the Kings!" Luger announced proudly and dropped the plexiglass on the gallery. Together, he and King Coopa hoisted up DeMozzio. He screamed and swung his arms wildly in a desperate attempt to get away, but today was Judgment Day.

"Pleeease, no, no, noooooo!" DeMozzio screamed so loudly the thing at the back of his throat shook. His fall to the ground below seemed slow, dramatic, and cinematic. There was a sickening noise, as he fell awkwardly on his neck, breaking it. it sounded like a chicken bone snapping in two. His blood quickly expanded around him and created a pool. He lay wide-eyed, tongue hanging out, and bone protruding from his neck.

King Coopa and Luger looked over the guardrail, staring down at DeMozzio. Luger nudged him with his elbow, signaling it was time to go. They recovered their pokers and ran off to handle their next kill.

***

Draco kicked one of the Kings of Thieves into the guardrail, his enemy's scream echoing as he fell to the cement floor below. Another King caught Draco off guard, stabbing him in the back. Draco bit down hard on his lip, choking back the pain, and spun around, only to be hit with another blow—this time, two vicious stabs to his side. The fire in his veins drove him forward; he slashed the throat of the King who attacked him, watching as his eyes bubbled and his hands instinctively clutched his gushing neck. Draco used the dying man as a human shield, shoving him toward the next attacker. The King's knife plunged into his comrade's chest, high on the left side, right in the heart.

With a savage growl, Draco rushed forward, ramming his human shield into the attacking King, pinning him against the bars of a cell. Growling, he stabbed him in the cheek twice, blood spurting in all directions. He then drove the blade into his eye, the sickening crunch of bone and cartilage filling the air.

"Aaaaaaah!" The King's scream was a symphony of agony, music to Draco's ears.

Draco shoved his human shield forward, sending both the dead man and the impaled King crashing to the tier. Panting, his eyes darted left and right. He saw more Kings of Thieves closing in on both sides of the gallery, their eyes gleaming with murderous intent, shanks ready to finish him. He knew he couldn't survive this.

Draco glanced over the guardrail, the drop to the cement floor below daunting, but it was his only shot. He tossed his shank aside and climbed over the rail. Holding onto the lower bar, he took one last look at the approaching Kings, who were racing down the stairs to catch him if he survived the fall.

Draco released his grip and plummeted. The impact was brutal, his leg bending in a way it shouldn't have as he crashed to the ground with a howl of pain. He tried to push through it, dragging himself toward his cell, his leg a throbbing mess of purple and red. He knew it was fractured, but there was no time to think about that now. The Kings were coming for him, and they were coming fast.

Just as the first of them reached him, Draco threw himself into his cell and slid the bars shut. He barely made it. The Kings were on him, arms snaking through the bars, shanks slashing wildly, desperately trying to slice him. Draco staggered back, feeling a sharp pain in his chest. He looked down and saw blood seeping through his shirt, a wound he hadn't noticed in the heat of the fight. Now that the adrenaline was wearing off, the pain was becoming all too real.

"Shit," Draco muttered, clutching his chest. He could feel the life draining out of him. By the time any medical help arrived, it would be too late. He knew it.

"Fuck it," he said aloud, trying to convince himself. "I've lived one hell of a life since I've been here. I can die without any regrets."

But then a voice cut through his thoughts, chilling him to the core.

"You're wrong, Papi. Your regret will be letting yo' youngin' fall right behind you," the voice taunted.

Draco looked up and saw Luger, King Coopa, and the other Kings standing calmly outside his cell, their knives glinting in the dim light.

"What the fuck are you talking about, moreno?" Draco spat, his anger masking the fear rising within him.

"When was the last time you hollered at cho Madukes? You know, to check on yo' baby boy?" Luger asked, a sinister smile playing on his lips.

Draco's blood ran cold. He scrambled to his contraband cellphone, dialing his mother's number with shaking hands. On the second ring, an unfamiliar voice answered.

"Mommy?" Draco's voice cracked, terror gripping his heart.

"Nah, you goya bean eatin' muthafucka, it ain't cha mommy," the voice sneered.

"Who is this?" Draco demanded, his voice shaking with fury and dread. He glanced at Luger, who was still smiling, enjoying every second of Draco's torment.

"This is the nigga that has the neck of yo' sweet, baby boy in his hands right now," the man said coldly. "And if you don't do as I say, I'm gonna twist it 'til I hear a pop. Ya dig?"

"Where's my mother?" Draco's face turned red as tears spilled from his eyes, his fear for his family overtaking him.

The man on the other end laughed, a chilling, maniacal sound that sent shivers down Draco's spine. "Madukes is kinda tied up right now, so she can't come to the phone if you know what I mean."

Draco's heart broke as he fought to stay composed. He closed his eyes, taking a deep breath to calm himself. "What do you want?" he asked, knowing he had no choice but to comply.

"I want chu to call whomever you hired to off King Chyna's old man and tell 'em to abort the fuckin' mission, asap," the man ordered. "You do that, and I'll leave yo' OG and ya seed how I found them."

"Okay," Draco whispered, his voice breaking as he looked at Luger's sadistic grin.

"You got three minutes, my nigga, and if you on some bullshit," the man threatened, "I'ma pop this lil' spic's neck like a gotdamn bottle of champagne."

Draco hung up, his hands trembling as he dialed Berrios. He ordered him to stand down, cancel the hit, and tell him to keep the money. His heart raced as he completed the call, praying it would be enough.

When he called back, the man confirmed that he'd followed orders, and Draco heard the unmistakable sound of keys jingling outside his cell. Luger, still grinning, held up the keys to Draco's cell and slowly unlocked it.

Draco knew his number was up. He plucked the tacked picture of his baby boy from the wall, kissed it, and held it close to his heart. As Luger and the Kings entered his cell, Draco closed his eyes, bracing himself for the end. He whispered a final goodbye to his son as they descended upon him, prepared to meet his Lord and Savior.

DeMozzio and Draco weren't the last to fall. Luger, King Coopa, and the Kings turned on the remaining members of their faction who dared to rise against the slaughter of their top dawgs.

The betrayal was swift and ruthless, they cut down anyone who stood in their way.

The jail became a battlefield. The last of the resistance crumbled, leaving pools of blood on the cold cement floor of those who realized too late that they had chosen the wrong side.

When the dust finally settled, the bodies of the defiant lay scattered, their lifeless eyes staring blankly at the ceiling, never to challenge those who represented the crown again. Those who survived the carnage, their courage drained and their spirits broken, bloodied but alive, bowed their heads in submission, recognizing that they were in the presence of something far greater than themselves—the Kings of Thieves.

Berrios slammed his hand on the alarm clock, silencing its shrill ring. He sat up in bed, his body heavy with the weight of what the night held. He stretched, yawned, and staggered to the bathroom, where he stripped down and twisted the dials of the shower. The blast of hot water jolted him awake, but it did nothing to wash away the dread gnawing at his insides. He lathered the washcloth with soap, scrubbing his skin as if he could cleanse himself of the dark task that lay ahead.

His face reflected in the bathroom mirror was a picture of torment. It wasn't his job that had him on edge—he loved being a nurse. But tonight, he was tasked with something that went against every fiber of his being: ending the life of one of his patients. His digital watch was set with the precise date and time for the hit. The only way out was a call from the man who had ordered the murder. If the phone didn't ring by the appointed hour, Berrios knew he had to go through with it.

The thought of killing someone shook Berrios to his core. He wasn't a killer; he wasn't built for it. But the image of his son, Zayden, filled his heart and steeled his resolve. There was nothing he wouldn't do for the seven-year-old who looked at him like a superhero. Berrios would be damned if he spent every day saving strangers but couldn't save his own child's life.

After dressing, Berrios grabbed his lunch bag and kissed his sleeping wife and son goodbye. Standing in the doorway of Zayden's room, he whispered, "Everything I do, I do it for you, son," before shutting the door softly and heading down the hallway.

As he glanced at his digital watch, the countdown was relentless—four hours, thirty-six minutes, and forty-seven seconds before he had to do the unthinkable. He decided to take the long route to the hospital, hoping—praying—that he would get the call to abort the mission.

Berrios arrived at the hospital half an hour late, breaking nearly twelve years of perfect attendance. But he didn't care. He'd rather be late than live with the stain of someone's blood on his soul. As he clocked in, stashed his lunch in the fridge, and began his rounds, his colleagues noticed his uncharacteristic silence. The usual warmth and humor in his demeanor were gone, replaced by a heavy, brooding presence. They knew better than to pry, leaving him to wrestle with his demons in peace.

Sitting in the break room, Berrios picked at his lunch, his mind a million miles away. A fly crawled on his salami sandwich, but he barely noticed. He'd lost his appetite after a few bites, his heart racing as the alarm on his watch began to beep. It was time. His lunch break was over, and the moment he dreaded had arrived.

He stood slowly, discarded the remnants of his meal, and clocked back in. With his supplies in hand, he headed to Trick's room. The police officer stationed outside greeted him, but Berrios could only muster a weak smile in return. His mind was focused on the task ahead. As the officer flirted with a nurse's aide, Berrios knew this was his chance.

His hands trembled as he reached into his pocket and pulled out the syringe disguised as a pen. His heart pounded in his chest, and tears welled up in his eyes as he whispered a plea for forgiveness. He brought the syringe closer to Trick's vein, his entire body trembling with the weight of what he was about to do.

Suddenly, his phone rang, shattering the tense silence. Berrios nearly jumped out of his skin. Fumbling, he pulled out his phone and saw the name "Manny" flash on the screen—Draco. His heart pounded as he answered with a shaky voice.

"Yeah... I'm with him right now. No, I haven't. Seriously? Are you sure? Okay...take care."

The call ended, and Berrios crumpled to his knees beside Trick's bed, sobbing uncontrollably. Relief and gratitude flooded through him as he whispered, "Thank you, God... thank you..."

The nurse's aide rushed into the room, followed closely by the officer, his hand resting on his holstered gun, ready for anything. But what they found was not violence—just a man, broken and weeping, his soul spared from the abyss he had nearly plunged into.

***

Jayvon's fight with Neo left him partially blind in his left eye. He looked at his handicap as a blessing. He still had his life, and one good eye to watch his wife push his daughter out into the world—and that was good enough for him.

Chrissy's pregnancy progressed smoothly, and Jayvon was by her side every step of the way. They attended ultrasounds and shared dreams of their future. The gang supported them, becoming a tighter unit, bound not just by crime but by family.

One evening, as they all gathered for dinner, Jayvon raised a toast. "To the family," he said, his voice full of emotion. "And to the future. We've been through a lot, but we've got each other, and that's what matters."

They all raised their glasses, clinking them together. "To the family," they echoed.

***

As Chrissy's due date approached, the mansion buzzed with activity. Jayvon took on a more protective role, ensuring Chrissy was comfortable and had everything she needed. The nursery became a project of love, with everyone contributing.

Chyna painted the walls a soothing pastel color, while Bag Man assembled the crib. Augustus and Jayvon hung up decorations, and Chrissy supervised, her eyes gleaming joyiously.

"I can't believe we're going to be parents," Chrissy said one evening, resting her hand on her growing belly.

Jayvon smiled, placing a kiss on her forehead. "You're going to be an amazing mother. I can't wait to meet our lil' girl."

Chrissy's eyes filled with tears. "And you're going to be the best father. I know it."

***

The night Chrissy went into labor was filled with excitement and tension. Jayvon, heart-pounding with fear and anticipation, rushed her to the hospital. The gang waited anxiously in the waiting room.

Hours later, a nurse emerged, smiling. "Congratulations, Jayvon. You have a healthy baby girl."

Jayvon felt a wave of relief and joy wash over him. He hurried to Chrissy's side and found her cradling their baby girl. Tears slid down his cheeks as he took in the sight of his tiny, perfect child.

"Oh, my God, she's…she's beautiful," he whispered, kissing Chrissy's cheek. "You did amazing, Doll."

Chrissy, exhausted but elated, smiled. "She's perfect, Von. Just like her daddy."

As Jayvon took Jayla into his arms, he felt his heart swell with love. "Welcome to the world, Princess Jayla," he whispered. "We're going to take such good care of you."

***

Months later

Jayvon looked down at his daughter, cradled in his arms, and felt an overwhelming sense of purpose. He had promised to protect his family, and he intended to keep that promise. He knew the road ahead wouldn't be easy, but with Chrissy, Jayla, and his loyal crew by his side, he felt ready to face whatever obstacles life threw at him.

Jayvon, standing in the nursery watching Jayla sleep, whispered, "I'm gonna make sure you have the best life, lil' mama. You, your mom—all of us."

***

Trick slowly stirred awake from his coma, the fog rolling back from his brain. Groaning, he peeled his eyes open and squinted against the harsh fluorescent lights of the hospital room. As his vision cleared, he took in his surroundings. The sterile white walls, the steady beep of the heart monitor, and the unmistakable scent of antiseptic all confirmed he was in a hospital.

He turned his head slightly and noticed a cop stationed at his door, alert and watchful. Trick's eyes moved to his wrist, feeling the cold metal before he saw it—a handcuff securing him to the guardrail of his bed. He sighed and dropped his head back against the pillow, smirking slightly. Despite the restraints and the constant surveillance, he was alive, and for that, he was thankful.

As he lay there, memories of the fight that landed him in this situation began to flood back. The clash with that nigga Draco, the intense battle with the Puerto Ricans, and the moment everything went black. He shifted slightly, feeling the ache in his muscles and the bandages covering his wounds. Though he had fought hard and had come out on the other side, he wasn't unscathed.

Trick's thoughts were interrupted by the soft creak of the door opening. His nurse, Berrios, walked in and glanced at the monitor. He then looked at Trick. He thought it was wild that not long ago he was playing God to him, having to choose to kill him or let him live.

Man, this is a crazy ass world we live in.

"Unc, it's good to see you're finally awake," Berrios said, checking his vitals. "You've been outta while."

"How long?" Trick croaked, his voice hoarse from disuse.

"A few weeks," Berrios replied, making a note on his clipboard. "You gave us quite the scare."

Trick nodded slightly, absorbing the information. *A few weeks. It felt like a lifetime and a moment all at once.* The words slowly formed in his mind as he looked at the nurse again.

"Thank you," he said quietly. "For taking care of me."

The nurse smiled warmly. "Just doing my job. You're lucky to be alive, you know. Not everyone gets a second chance."

Trick's smirk widened slightly. "Yeah, lucky me."

Trick didn't feel as lucky as some think he should be. Yeah, he had a second chance at life, but the remainder of that life would unfortunately be spent behind bars. The way he saw it, who the fuck would want to live a life like that?

***

Trick was deep into a game of Spades, eyes taking in the various faces of his opponents seated at the table. The dull hum of the prison's daily grind was a constant backdrop, but for Trick, the game was an escape—a brief reprieve from the cold, gray reality of his life behind bars.

"Trick!" a correctional officer called out, interrupting his concentration. Trick glanced up, irritation flickering across his face.

"You've got visitors," the officer said, motioning for him to follow.

Trick tossed down his cards, signaling the end of the game. His fellow inmates grumbled, but he paid them no mind. Visitors were rare, and he wasn't about to miss this one. He pushed back his chair and followed the officer through the labyrinth of concrete corridors, the sounds of prison life fading as they approached the visiting room.

When he entered, Trick's eyes immediately fell on Jayvon and Chrissy, seated at one of the tables. A smile broke across his face as he saw Chrissy holding a tiny bundle in her arms.

"Yo, whaddup, Scrap?" Trick greeted them, voice dripping genuine warmth.

"Sup, Pop?" Jayvon replied, throwing his head back.

Chrissy leaned forward, gently pulling back the blanket to reveal the cute face of their sleeping infant. "This is Jayla, your granddaughter."

Trick's eyes softened as he looked at the baby and a broad smile spread across his lips. "Man, she looks just like Chyna," he said, voice filled with pride. "She's beautiful."

Chrissy beamed, her motherly pride evident. "She's got his eyes, doesn't she?"

"Yeah, she does," Trick agreed, still gazing at Jayla. For a moment, the harsh reality of prison life seemed to melt away, replaced by the simple joy of seeing his granddaughter.

After a few minutes of cooing over the baby, they moved on to talk about life on the outside.

"How you been holding up, Pop?" Jayvon asked, leaning back in his chair.

"Same ol', same ol'," Trick replied with a shrug. "You know how it is in here—ain't nothin' change. But it's good to see y'all doing awight."

"Yeah, we're good," Chrissy said. "I mean, it's tough, but we're getting by."

Jayvon nodded in agreement. "We've been making it work."

Trick listened intently, nodding along as they spoke. Hearing about the life he was missing out on was bittersweet, but at the same time, it gave him hope. He wasn't forgotten. His family was out there, living, and growing, and they hadn't given up on him.

"I'm glad to hear that," Trick said sincerely. "Y'all stay dangerous. And remember, there's nothin' more important than family."

Chrissy reached across the table, placing her hand over Trick's. "We know. And we're doing everything we can to keep this family together. We miss you."

"I miss y'all too," Trick replied. "But this, seeing my grandbaby, it makes it all a lil' easier. I'll be out one day, and we'll be together again. You just wait."

***

Mother Nature was in a good mood this Thursday afternoon. The sun spread its grace over the suburbs, granting a hot day with the occasional breeze.

Jayvon sat behind the wheel of his Mercedez-Benz station listening to satellite radio as he waited for Chrissy to strap the baby into the car seat. Kissing the sleeping child on her forehead, Chrissy hopped into the front passenger seat and her hubby pulled off.

Jayvon glanced at Chrissy's reflection in the passenger window. He could tell by the look on her face that she was in deep thought. He didn't bother prying because he knew she'd likely tell him she was fine like always. Chrissy was one of those types that would fill you in on what was going on with her when she felt the time was right. So getting her to say anything when she wasn't ready would be as troublesome as pulling a hippo's aching tooth. The best he could do was show her affection. Her love language was touch. She adored being showered in kisses and other intimate forms of affection.

Jayvon gently picked up Chrissy's hand, kissed it, and held it in his lap. She looked at him with a grin on her lips and twinkling eyes.

"I love you, Doll." He told her.

"I love you just as much. Maybe even more." She replied.

"You wanna bet?" She smiled harder and shook her head. "Good. 'Cause that's one gamble you'd most definitely lose."

Chrissy kissed her palm and blew him a kiss. Then she focused her attention out of the window. She wasn't looking at anything particularly, but she was thinking about Josephine. And the night the shit hit the fan and everything transpired afterwards.

***

Josephine sat at the head of the dinner table, watching her five children devour their meal with the enthusiasm only kids could muster. Her baby daddy, Marcus, was in the middle of a funny story, making everyone laugh. Just as she was about to take a bite of her food, her cellphone rang. The screen displayed Chrissy's name. Josephine hesitated, a frown creasing her forehead.

"Don't you think you should answer that?" Marcus said, pausing his story. "Maybe she changed her mind and wants to give you your cut of the money we helped steal."

Josephine gave it a quick thought and then picked up the phone. "Hello?"

"Josephine!" Chrissy's voice was frantic. "You need to take your family and get out of the house right now! Finesse is after you!"

Before Josephine could respond, the front door burst open, and goons armed with AR-15s with suppressors stormed inside. Marcus sprang up from the table, but a short burst of gunfire sent him crashing back into his chair, his body lifeless.

The children screamed, their wails piercing the air. Josephine stood frozen, her mind unable to process the horror unfolding before her. One of the goons speed-walked up to her and punched her in the face, knocking her out cold. She crumpled to the floor, her cellphone lying beside her with Chrissy's voice still frantically calling her name.

***

Josephine awoke to find herself gagged and duct-taped to a chair inside the bathroom. Her eyes were glassy and pink from crying, and snot dripped from her nostrils. Two of Finesse's goons stood guard on either side of the door, their expressions blank and unfeeling. The sound of footsteps echoed down the hallway, and then Finesse strolled in, removing his suit jacket and rolling up his sleeves. An eye-patch covered his right eye socket, a reminder of the brutal world they lived in.

He knelt before Josephine, his gaze piercing. "You have the most beautiful children I've ever seen," he said softly. "I'd hate to do what I have in mind to them, but I will if you don't tell me where my money is."

Josephine's voice trembled as she swore, "I swear to God, some masked men jacked Chrissy's guy and his men for the money. I don't have it."

Finesse's expression hardened. "I'm not in the mood for stories, Josephine."

He signaled to one of his goons, who grabbed Josephine's youngest son and dragged him to the bathtub filled with water. The boy's terrified screams filled the small room as Finesse forced his head underwater. Josephine screamed and thrashed in her chair, trying desperately to break free.

"Stop it! Please!" she begged, tears streaming down her face. "He's just a child!"

But Finesse didn't relent. He held the boy underwater until the thrashing stopped and the last of the bubbles surfaced. With a cold efficiency, he laid the boy's lifeless body on the bathroom floor.

Josephine's remaining children were screaming and crying, their faces contorted with fear. Two of them ran to Josephine, hugging her tightly, while the other two tried to escape. The goons caught them easily, dragging them back into the room.

Finesse grabbed Josephine's daughter next, his grip unyielding. He looked Josephine in the eyes as he submerged the girl's head underwater. Her small body convulsed, fighting for breath, but it was no use. When she was still, he laid her beside her brother.

"Are you ready to tell me where Chrissy is?" he asked, his voice devoid of emotion.

Josephine sobbed, shaking her head. "I don't know where she is! I swear I don't know!"

Finesse sighed, a look of mock disappointment on his face. "You brought this on yourself."

He pulled another of her children away from her, ignoring their cries and pleas. He repeated the brutal process, drowning each child until they were all lying lifeless on the floor. Josephine's face was soaked with tears, her eyes vacant and hollow.

After drowning the last child, Finesse knelt before Josephine again. "Tell me where Chrissy is," he demanded, his tone growing more impatient.

But Josephine was beyond words. She began softly singing The Mockingbird song, her voice quivering and broken. Finesse's anger turned to confusion as he tried to make sense of the lyrics spilling from her lips.

"Hello? Is anyone home?" Finesse asked, snapping his fingers and waving his hand in front of her face. There was no response. Josephine was incoherent, lost in her grief and despair.

Disappointed, Finesse shook his head and slung his jacket over his shoulder. As he walked out of the bathroom, one of the goons asked, "What do you want us to do with her?"

"Leave her be," Finesse replied, his voice devoid of emotion. "She's not worth killing at this point."

The goons nodded and followed Finesse out of the room, leaving Josephine alone with the bodies of her children. She continued to sing, her voice a haunting echo in the otherwise silent house.

The house was eerily quiet after Finesse and his goons left. Josephine's mind was a whirlwind of despair, and her body was paralyzed with grief. She continued to sing The Mockingbird song, her voice faltering as the reality of her situation sank in.

Outside, the sound of sirens began to grow louder. Chrissy had called the police after hearing the commotion over the phone, hoping they could save Josephine and her family. But it was too late. The officers who arrived were met with a scene of unspeakable horror.

They found Josephine still duct-taped to the chair, her eyes vacant, and her voice hoarse from singing. The bodies of her children lay beside her, a grim testament to the brutality they had endured. The officers moved quickly, freeing Josephine from her bonds and trying to comfort her, but she was unresponsive, trapped in a world of her own making.

In the days that followed, the story of Josephine's tragedy spread throughout the community. Friends and neighbors were horrified by the violence that had been inflicted on her family. Vigils were held, candles were lit, and prayers were offered, but nothing could erase the pain and loss that Josephine felt.

Chrissy tried to visit Josephine in the hospital, but Josephine's mind was shattered, and she didn't recognize anyone. She remained in a catatonic state, her eyes blank and her voice silent.

Finesse and his goons disappeared, leaving no trace behind. The police launched an investigation, but they couldn't find any leads. Finesse had slipped through their fingers and left a trail of devastation in his wake.

***

Josephine was moved to a long-term care facility. She showed no signs of improvement, her mind lost in the traumatic events of that night. Her room was filled with pictures of her children, a reminder of the family she had lost.

One day, a nurse entered her room with a small, battered book. "Your sister dropped this off," she said softly, placing the book in Josephine's lap.

"Sister?" Josephine's forehead wrinkled. She was an only child so she didn't know who the nurse was referring to.

"Yeah. Your sister Chrissy," the nurse told her, "Said she got it from your house. Found it while she was packing your things. Thought it might bring you some comfort."

"Is she still here?"

"No. I told her you weren't up to seeing anyone so she left." the nurse said. "I could try to catch up with her if you'd like."

"No. I don't want her to see me like this." Josephine replied. "I'll make sure to see her next time. When I don't look like the hell I've been through." she picked at her hair. She looked like a crazed cat lady who never left the house and smelled funny.

"Okay. Well, I'll leave you to it," the nurse left the rec room where Josephine was sitting with other patients. Everyone was watching television and chatting about a whole bunch of nothing.

Josephine was one of the only ones who was quiet and barely paying attention to the daytime soap opera.

Josephine's fingers traced the cover of the book, her eyes slowly focusing on it. It was a collection of lullabies she used to sing to her children. Tears welled up in her eyes as she opened the book and began to read.

For the first time in a long time, Josephine felt a flicker of something she thought she had lost forever: hope. It was a small spark, but it was enough to remind her that she was still alive and *that she had a reason to keep going. She began to hum the tune of The Mockingbird song, her voice trembling but steady.*

At that moment, Josephine knew that she would never forget the horrors of that night, but she also knew that she had to find a way to keep living. For her children and herself.

***

The weeks following the discovery of the book were filled with small but significant improvements. Josephine began to respond to her surroundings more, recognizing familiar faces and engaging in simple activities. The staff at the care facility noticed her progress and provided additional support to help her heal.

Chrissy continued to visit Josephine regularly. She brought flowers and read to her. Slowly but surely, Josephine began to emerge from her shell.

***

Jayvon pulled up outside the facility that housed Josephine. Chrissy kissed him and walked inside. She signed in, checked in her purse, and placed the sticky visitor badge on her chest. An orderly led her to Josephine who was sitting at the dining room table. She was looking through the book Chrissy left on her last visit.

"Here she is. Be sure to sign out at the front desk once you're ready to leave," the orderly told her before walking out.

Nodding, Chrissy pulled a chair from the dining room table and sat beside Josephine.

"Hey, sis, long time no see. I'm glad you let me see you this time," Chrissy said as she swept the strands of hair out of Josephine's face, tucking them behind her ear. It was like Chrissy was a ghost. The way Josephine ignored her and continued to flip through the pages of the book. "They treating you alright in here?" Josephine didn't say anything. "Huh?" Still nothing.

Chrissy went on talking to Josephine. It was like talking to a plant to her. Seeing she wasn't going to get a word out of her, she sat quietly for twenty minutes, hoping she'd get some sort of correspondence but she didn't.

Chrissy glanced at her watch and then back up at Josephine. "I'm gonna go ahead and get outta here, girl. I got the hubbs and the baby waiting out in the parking lot for me,"—she rose from her chair— "I'll be back to see you next week. Maybe you'll be in the mood to talk then. Love you." she kissed her temple and grasped her shoulder affectionately. She'd gotten halfway to the door when Josephine finally said something.

"I miss them...I miss my babies," Josephine confessed, teardrops dripping from her eyes. She swept them away quickly. "Sometimes I think I hear them playing in here. I run through this place, checking everywhere, looking for them...but they're not here...they're gone...gone forever..." her voice cracked and she brokedown sobbing, body trembling uncontrollably.

    Chrissy rushed over and hugged her tightly. Tears burst from her eyes as she listened to Chrissy's sobs. "Go ahead, mamas, cry for 'em...cry for yo' babies, let it all out...cleanse your soul of all the hurt...all the pain...all the confusion...all of it." Chrissy encouraged, rubbing Josephine's back comfortingly.

    With each passing day, Josephine grew stronger. She participated in therapy sessions and began to eat more. Eventually, she was well enough to be released from the hospital. She lived with Chrissy and Jayvon until she felt she could live on her own. She stopped working at gentlemen's clubs, landed a gig at the post office, and met a new guy. As of today, Josephine is married and expecting her second child.

***

    Neo, feeling the warmth of family and camaraderie, trained tirelessly under his father's guidance. Luka taught him not just the art of combat, but also the importance of wisdom and strategy.

    Jayvon, balancing his role as a new father and leader, spent many evenings discussing plans with Luka. They talked about fortifying their defenses, expanding their influence, and ensuring their enemies could never harm their loved ones again.

    One evening, as the sun dipped below the horizon, Jayvon stood on the balcony with Chrissy, Jayla cradled in his arms.

"We've been through so much, but we're still standing," Chrissy said softly, her voice filled with pride.

Jayvon kissed her forehead. "And we'll keep standing, no matter what comes our way. We've got each other, and that's all we need."

Jayvon had fought for his family and his friends, and he had won. Together, they would face whatever challenges lay ahead, united by an unbreakable bond.

***

The future was bright for Jayvon, Neo, and their families. With their newfound alliances, they knew they could face anything that came their way.

Neo, now fully integrated into his family, felt a sense of belonging he had never known before. His siblings, eager to make up for lost time, shared stories, laughter, and dreams for the future. Together, they trained, celebrated, and grew stronger.

Jayvon, Chrissy, and Jayla were embraced as part of this extended family. They found peace and happiness in the simple moments of everyday life, knowing they were surrounded by love and support.

***

As Neo stood with his family one evening, watching the sunset over their estate, he felt a profound sense of peace. He had found his place in the world, surrounded by love and support.

As the stars began to twinkle in the night sky, Neo knew that with his family by his side, there was nothing they couldn't overcome. Their lives were theirs to shape, and together, they would create a legacy.

Jayvon walked up beside Neo and placed a hand on his shoulder, looking around the acres of land owned by his family.

"Everythang the light touches," he repeated the famous line from The Lion King before busting up laughing with his newest friend.

"You've got jokes, man." Neo smiled, extending his flute of champagne.

"To new friends and new beginnings."

"To new friends and new beginnings." Jayvon smiled, touching his flute to his.

They swallowed what was left in their glasses and placed them on top of the armrest.

"Now, about that rematch," Neo turned to him, grinning.

"Ready when you are, big dawg." Jayvon grinned.

***

Jayvon and Neo stood under the moonlight, bare barefoot. They stretched their arms, legs, and backs and rolled their heads around their shoulders, preparing to fight. With a burst of uncontrollable energy, they charged at each other screaming like warriors and leaping high up, legs extended to attack.

THE END...MOTHAFUCKAZ!!!

My self-published books

BLOODY KNUCKLES 1-3
THE DEVIL WEARS TIMBS 1-7
ME AND MY HITTAZ 1-6
THE LAST REAL NIGGA ALIVE 1-3
FANGEANCE
A HOOD NIGGA'S BLUES
A SOUTH CENTRAL LOVE AFFAIR
GOD BLESS THE TRAPPERS 1-3
THE DOPEMAN'S BODYGUARD 1-2
FEAR MY GANGSTA 1-5
THESE SCANDALOUS STREETS 1-3

My books published under LDP

KING OF THE TRENCHES 1-3
THE REALEST KILLAZ 1-3
THE LAST OF THE OG's 1-3
MONEY HUNGRY DEMONS 1-3

Coming Soon

THERE'S NO PLACE IN HEAVEN FOR THUGS
THEY MADE ME AN ANIMAL

www.ingramcontent.com/pod-product-compliance
Lightning Source LLC
LaVergne TN
LVHW021815060526
838201LV00058B/3405